Hideout at Mender's Crossing

The ghost town of Mender's Crossing was the ideal base for a gang of outlaws to operate from without interference. Then, a group of soldiers are killed defending a gold-train and the army calls upon special operator Steve Landers to investigate.

Now, Landers must face not only the gang but land baron Hal Clegg, whose hired mercenaries are driving independent ranchers off their land. He will need nerves of steel if he is to succeed when he is so heavily outnumbered. Can he cheat the odds and win?

By the same author

Bowie of the Alamo
Day of Violence
Guntrail to Condor

Hideout at Mender's Crossing

John Glasby

ROBERT HALE · LONDON

First published in Great Britain 2010

ISBN 978-0-7090-8939-1

Robert Hale Limited
Clerkenwell House
Clerkenwell Green
London EC1R 0HT

www.halebooks.com

Typeset by
Derek Doyle & Associates, Shaw Heath
Printed and bound in Great Britain by
CPI Antony Rowe, Chippenham and Eastbourne

1

HIDEOUT

Situated near the northern edge of the infamous Willard Flats, Mender's Crossing was little more than a dusty trail with a couple of dozen wooden buildings on either side. It was now a ghost town – a home to sidewinders and desert lizards with only buzzards in the sky drifting like rags of black cloth in the cloudless heavens. It slumbered in eerie silence, a stark reminder of days long gone. Once, long before the war between the North and South, it had been a staging post for the pony express and a small township had grown up around it. But even the hardy pioneers soon found it impossible to live in that harsh region and had pulled out, until now it was completely deserted.

Except for three men and their mounts. For these men, James Butler, Will Iliff and Matt Minter, it provided them with the ideal hiding-place.

The railroad, with its rich pickings, lay only fifteen miles to the north. Within an hour's ride were several small towns where they could strike without warning. Once they were clear of the town there were few men who dared to follow them into the infamous Flats.

There were even fewer now alive who could remember Mender's Crossing. Most folk now believed it to be nothing more than a myth, like the Valley of Gold which was said to exist somewhere far to the south.

Butler and Minter were seated at the small table in the once sumptuous saloon that they had made their headquarters, playing poker. At the window, Iliff stared out across the miles of empty, barren land, struggling to quell the mounting impatience in his mind. They had been holed up in this god-forsaken place now for more than two weeks while Minter made up his mind where they would strike next. Sometimes he wondered whether Minter wasn't getting too old for this business. It needed someone who was willing to take a chance to run this small band.

He swatted angrily at a fly buzzing against the dust-smeared glass. It was true that their last venture had been a catastrophe. Somehow the law had received prior warning and a whole band of armed citizens was waiting for them. Men with rifles had been posted all the way along either side of the street and they'd had no chance to hit the bank. Only sheer luck and quick thinking had enabled them to get out of town and escape by the skin of their teeth. That had been the first time they'd returned empty-handed. Whatever

Minter had in mind, he seemed determined that the same thing would not happen again. The trouble with Minter was that he always played his cards close to his chest. Until he'd worked things through he never gave any indication of the thoughts passing through his mind.

Turning sharply, Iliff addressed the tall man seated at the table. 'How much longer are we goin' to stick around here, Matt? Two weeks in this hellhole, sittin' around doin' nothing is gettin' on my nerves. If you've got no ideas then just say so.'

'We stay here until I give the order to ride out,' growled Minter. His gaze remained fixed on the cards in his hand. 'If you don't like the way I handle things you know what you can do. Take your share of what we've already got and ride out now. But if you do, I'm givin' you fair warnin'. You keep your mouth shut about this place. Spill anythin' about this hideout and Jim and I will find you wherever you try to hide. You got that?'

Butler tossed his cards on to the table. 'Maybe Will's right, Matt. Besides, we're now runnin' short o' grub. I've been thinkin' we should—'

Laying his cards down on the table, Minter scooped the pile of dollar bills towards him and snapped angrily, 'That's the trouble with you, both o' you. You think too much. Whenever one o' you rides into town for food, you don't use your eyes and ears. Sometimes I reckon you must be gettin' moonstruck over some woman in Fenton. If either of you has that idea in mind forget it. We're in this business for the money and for as long as I say so.'

'And I suppose you use your eyes and ears when you're in town.' Iliff moved away from the window and threw himself down in the vacant chair, his swarthy features creased into angry, frustrated lines.

Minter nodded. 'That's right, I do. You want some action? Then you'll get it and soon.'

'What's that supposed to mean?' Butler leaned forward in his chair, suddenly interested. 'Have you picked up somethin'?'

'I've heard enough to know that there's a trainload o' gold blocks comin' from back East. I reckon there's enough gold aboard that train for all of us. And we're goin' to take it.'

'You're sure of all this?' Iliff muttered. He sounded dubious. 'I ain't heard anythin' about a trainload o' gold.'

'It was easy enough to get the information out o' one of the men workin' at the railroad depot. All it needed was a few drinks in the saloon in town. There's nothin' like free whiskey to loosen a man's tongue.'

'So when is it comin?' Butler demanded.

'The day after tomorrow. It's due to arrive in town at noon so we hit it before it gets there.'

There was a hint of suspicion in Iliff's gruff voice as he asked, 'So you've known about this for three days, Matt. Why didn't you mention it before? Or were you plannin' on gettin' it all for yourself?'

Minter half-rose from his chair. His right hand dipped towards the gun at his waist. His hard features reddened with fury at the implication in Iliff's words.

Then he relaxed. 'I want no more talk like that,' he said with a note of menace in his voice. 'Either we all work together, or we're finished. You understand?'

Iliff pressed his lips into a tight line. For a moment he seemed on the point of arguing. Then he sat back and nodded. 'All right, Matt. I'll go along with you. Let's hear what you've got to say.'

'Good. Now let's work out how we're goin' to do this.'

'You're sure this *hombre*'s information can be relied on?' Butler asked.

'I'm damned sure. He'd no idea who he was talkin' to and he was drunk enough to be tellin' the truth.'

'And where's this gold headed?' Iliff queried.

'It's army gold being shipped to Fort Leveridge. That being the case, it's sure to be on time and we can expect it to be well-guarded.'

'It sounds risky to me.' Iliff looked dubious. 'I don't like the idea o' takin' on the army. Holdin' up a bank is one thing, but this is mighty different.'

'They won't be expectin' any trouble. That means we'll have the advantage of surprise.' Minter took a piece of paper from his pocket and spread it out on the table in front of him. 'This is the way I figure it.'

He traced out the line he had drawn on the crude map. 'This is the railroad. Seven miles east o' town there's this sharp bend and it's right on the edge of a steep upgrade. The train will have to travel slowly at that point. Furthermore, there are rocks on either side to provide us with plenty o' cover.'

'It looks fine to me,' Butler interjected.

Gruffly, Iliff muttered, 'Except for one thing you seem to have overlooked.'

'Oh, and what's that?'

'The men in charge o' that gold shipment are no fools. They ain't ordinary lawmen. All o' them are soldiers and they'll expect word o' this might get around and they'll have figured that if any attack is goin' to be made on that train, that's exactly where it'll be. Take my word for it, they'll be ready for anything.'

Minter pulled a wad of tobacco from his pocket, bit off a piece, and chewed noisily on it. Speaking around it, he went on harshly, 'Not if we attack 'em twice.'

Both of his companions looked perplexed. 'Are you plumb loco?' Butler looked up from the deck of cards he was shuffling absently. 'Why do that? Surely we'd be runnin' twice the risk?'

Minter jabbed his forefinger at the paper. 'Here,' he said sharply, 'the line runs straight for more'n ten miles before they reach that bend. There are places there where we can conceal ourselves, fire off a few shots and then take off. But we have to make it look like a real attack and they've beaten us off.'

'And you reckon that by doin' that, they won't expect us to hit them again.'

'That's the way I figure it.' Minter folded the map and pushed it back into his pocket. 'We'll go over all o' the details tomorrow just so that both o' you know exactly what to do.'

It was in the dark hour before the dawn, two days later,

when the three men rode out of Mender's Crossing and headed north. For some ten miles they had to ride across the alkali, where nothing grew but brittle sage and a few scattered clumps of Spanish sword. Apart from themselves, the only things that moved in the silence were the occasional scorpion and the large tumbleweeds rolling aimlessly over the wasteland. The dawn was just brightening in the east when they left the badlands behind them. Now they were riding through more dense vegetation.

Somewhere in the distance to their left was the small town of Fenton. Ahead of them was the single track of the railroad. The sun was just lifting clear of the eastern horizon when they sighted it. Iliff and Butler reined up their mounts, sitting high in the saddle as they ran their gaze over it.

A tall bluff hemmed in the track on the far side. Here the steel rails bent in a sharp curve, just as Minter had intimated, with a steep upgrade leading into it from the east.

Butler gave a brief nod. 'Seems you were right, Matt. This sure is the ideal spot to hit that train. You figurin' we should block the line here?'

'That's the idea. It shouldn't be too difficult. A charge o' gunpowder will bring half o' that bluff down on to the track.' He patted the large wooden barrels on either side of him. 'We also lay some along the line between the rails.'

'You thinkin' of blowing up the train as well?' Surprise edged Iliff's voice.

'I am. Apart from finishin' off most of those soldier

boys guardin' the train, it'll make it easier to get inside the vans for those strongboxes. Now let's get to work. Everything has to be ready by the time that train gets here.'

Sliding from his mount he took down the gunpowder, then rummaged inside his saddle-bag, bringing out lengths of fuse. 'This should be enough to bring down those rocks.'

He signalled to Butler. 'I want you up there with me.'

To Iliff, he said sharply. 'You stay here and keep watch. I'm not expectin' any trouble but I don't intend to take any unnecessary chances.'

Iliff moved his mount a little further from the track and watched the terrain on both sides as the two men pulled themselves up the rockface, clutching at hand- and footholds as they worked their way to the top. Working carefully, Minter located a large cleft in the rock. He eased the explosive gently into it.

Once this was done he inserted the fuse, making sure it was secure before letting the rest drop down on to the track below him. Slowly, he and Butler worked their way back down.

'Now get back out o' the way,' he ordered, 'and make sure the horses don't bolt.'

He waited until the others had retreated away from the track, then he struck a match, lighting the end of the fuse. He turned and ran back to the others, crouching down behind a line of rocks.

Three minutes later the explosive detonated with a violent explosion, to be followed by the grinding rumble of rocks avalanching on to the rails. Minter waited for a full five minutes before pushing himself upright and surveying the result of their handiwork. Around them, the dust and fumes settled slowly.

His two companions came to stand beside him as he nodded his head in satisfaction. The track was completely blocked by tons of rock and stone.

'Good. The engineer on that train won't see any o' that until he rounds the bend yonder.'

Butler laughed harshly. 'By that time it'll be too late. So what do we do now?'

'We get those smaller barrels of gunpowder you've been carryin', Will, and place them along the centre of the track. Then link them up and run the fuse across the rocks so that we can blow them from over there.' He indicated a tall mass of jumbled rocks. 'Make sure you thread the fuse beneath the rail, otherwise the train will crush it. Once we've done that there'll be plenty of time to ride east and find ourselves a place where we can hit the train with rifle fire.'

It was over half an hour later before Minter was satisfied that the explosive was in the correct position and the fuses were all linked up.

'Who's goin' to fire that explosive once the train gets here?' Iliff enquired.

'Either of you like to volunteer?' Minter asked.

When both men shook their heads he said grimly, 'I thought not. I'll do that while you two take up positions on this side of the track so that we can hit the soldier boys from both sides.'

Without a further word he swung into the saddle and waited as the other two did likewise. Turning their mounts, they headed east, following the track. At the bottom of the steep gradient the gleaming rails ran straight across the open country, stretching away as far as the eye could see.

For a few miles the track passed through flat, open country with no hint of concealment on either side. Minter cast a quick glance at the sun, then checked his watch. 'Another four hours before that train gets here,' he called. 'And remember. Once we hightail it from here we make it straight back to that bend. I reckon we can be sure the train won't stop here once we ride off. We have to be in position, and ready, before it does. You both got that?'

Both of his companions nodded their heads. Ahead of them the tracks continued in an almost perfectly straight line. On either side the land remained bare and open. Not until they had ridden a further three miles did they come across rougher country.

Riding a little way ahead of the others, Minter suddenly hauled hard on the reins and brought his mount to a sliding halt. 'This looks as good a place as any,' he called over his shoulder. 'It's further away from that bend than I'd like but that can't be helped.' He dropped from his mount and indicated the high jumble of rocks that bordered the track.

Both of his companions dismounted. 'What do we do now?' Butler asked gruffly.

'We wait. It'll be another three hours or so before that train comes into sight. Then we let them have it with rifle fire, enough to make 'em believe it's a real attack. Then we pull out and head back to the bend as fast as we can.'

The three men stretched themselves out on the bare rock. Squinting up at the blazing disc of the sun, Minter tilted his hat forward over his eyes, closing them as if he meant to sleep.

The hours passed with a painful slowness, each minute that ticked by heightening the tension in all of them. At intervals, one of them would get to his feet and peer into the hazy distance. At last Minter stood up and checked his watch. 'If it's on time it should be here in ten minutes or so,' he said sharply. 'You'd better get into position. And remember, this has got to look as if we intend to take the train right here.'

Twelve minutes later Iliff spotted the plume of black smoke in the distance. Minter glanced at his watch again. 'They're almost five minutes late accordin' to my reckoning,' he muttered. 'Knowing how the military are, I figure they might try to make up some time. That means we have to ride fast to get back to the bend if we're to make it in time. Once I give the signal to pull out, be ready to mount up.'

Quickly, they took up their positions among the rocks. Now it was possible to hear the train. As it came closer they noticed a small number of men in uniform outside the coaches, holding on to the sides.

Minter smiled grimly to himself. This was going to be like shooting ducks at a fairground. He checked his rifle and waited.

The locomotive passed alongside where they were

concealed. The hissing of steam and the clanking of the connecting rods almost deafened them. In the noise the sound of their fire was lost.

Three of the soldiers jerked and fell as the bullets found their mark, dropping on to the side of the track, not knowing what had hit them. A fourth managed to get off a couple of shots before he too died and fell. Someone inside the train yelled an order. Almost at once the glass in several of the windows was shattered, smashed by rifle butts as the men on the train suddenly realized they were under attack.

Two men pulled themselves up on to the roof of the van, throwing themselves flat and firing swiftly into the rocks. Iliff pulled his head down as a couple of slugs ricocheted off the rock and whined thinly into the distance.

A few yards away, Minter ducked instinctively as the soldiers' fire came dangerously close. The train had almost passed them and was now picking up speed. Two more men had appeared in the observation car at the rear and begun firing.

They continued firing for another five minutes before Minter yelled, 'Time to get out o' here.' He pushed himself to his feet, flinched as a slug passed within an inch of his head. Doubled over, he raced for his mount and swung himself swiftly into the saddle. Butler and Iliff did likewise, digging spurs into their horses' flanks and racing away from the track.

They rode until they were out of sight of the railroad track and then swung north, pushing their mounts to the limit. Once the bend came into sight they reined up and slid quickly from the saddle. All of them knew that this was going to be the tricky part of the whole operation. Everything had to be carried out with split-second timing.

Swiftly, they led their horses out of sight. While Minter climbed to the top of the bluff on the far side of the track, the other two took up their positions among the rocks.

This time they had only a few minutes to wait before the sound of the approaching train reached them. From his vantage point, Minter waited. He had already estimated the time it would take for the fuse to burn through to the waiting explosive.

Holding his breath, he waited with tension mounting swiftly inside him. This would require everything to go right the first time. They wouldn't get a second chance if something went wrong. The locomotive had now reached the start of the steep upgrade and he could hear the engineer giving it more steam as it began to climb.

He struck a match off the nearby rock and waited for a further second. Then he applied the flame to the fuse. Moving more slowly now, the train approached the bend. Crouching down, hoping that the other two men had taken up their correct positions, he glimpsed the black shape of the locomotive as it rounded the sharp curve.

The engineer must have spotted the obstruction on the tracks in virtually the same moment, because an instant later there came the shrill screech of the brakes being applied.

Sparks flew in all directions from beneath the wheels. Confused shouting reached him as Minter pressed himself harder against the rock, covering his ears. There came a resounding crash as the locomotive smashed into the obstacle, followed ten seconds later by the blast of the explosive. The train was lifted several feet into the air by the force of the explosion. Twisted lengths of metal rail flew in all directions.

The reverberating echoes of the blast were still fading into the distance when there came a further crash as the wreckage of the engine and coaches smashed back on to the torn-up track. Minter could hear the shrill screams of injured and dying men.

A few of the accompanying men guarding the gold were still on their feet, however, having miraculously survived much of the blast, but already Butler and Iliff had opened fire from the opposite side of the track. Slowly, however, the volume of the return gunfire was diminishing. The explosive had done its work well.

Raising his head slowly, Minter saw two men in uniform staggering along the track. Swiftly, he pulled the Colt from its holster and pulled the trigger twice. Both men fell without a sound. He waited for a full minute before thrusting himself to his feet and sliding down the rocks.

Steam was still hissing from the locomotive, which now lay on its side, but he paid no attention to this or to the yells and screams of the dying. Running quickly along the track, he reached the last coach but one. It lay tilted on its side, the steel doors blown apart leaving a gaping hold in the side.

A moment later Iliff and Butler came running towards him.

'All right.' Minter pointed. 'You two get inside there and pass out those bags and boxes.'

The two men pulled themselves inside the coach and began lowering the contents down to Minter.

At last Iliff called, 'That's the last o' them, Matt. We've got them all.'

'Good. Now let's get them loaded on to the horses and get away from here.' He gave the two men a hand as they pulled themselves from the wreckage.

Ten minutes later they had the bags tied to the saddles and were heading away from the scene of destruction.

2

DESPERATE MEASURES

Two days later and fifty miles to the west a lone rider approached the gates of Fort Leveridge. Steve Landers eyed the sentries on duty on the wall above the gates and guessed they were wondering just who he was and what business he had there.

The gates were shut but as Steve rode up to them one of the watching sentries on the parapet called something to someone below. The gates swung open and he rode through, across the wide parade ground, towards the buildings on the far side. There was a hitching rail to which he tied the sorrel, then he climbed the wooden steps.

Two men with rifles stood on either side of the doorway. One of them came forward. 'Who do you wish to see, sir?' he asked.

'My name's Landers,' Steve told him. 'Major Anderson sent me a message asking me to get here as quickly as possible.'

'I'll take you to him, sir.' The man eyed Steve up and down for a moment and then turned smartly, opened the door, and motioned to Steve to follow him. They went along a wide passage towards the door at the far end. Steve's companion knocked twice, then thrust open the door.

The man who sat behind the desk near the window had iron-grey hair, a trim moustache, and light-blue eyes that drilled into Steve's as he walked forward.

The major got to his feet, shook hands, then motioned him to the chair in front of the desk. 'I'm mighty glad you managed to get here so quickly, Landers,' he said briskly. 'This may seem a strange request I'm making but there's a reason for it.'

'I gathered it had to be mighty important for you to drag me halfway across the state, Major.'

'Believe me, it is.' Anderson picked up a pipe from the desk and began stuffing brown strands of tobacco into it. He lit it, puffed furiously on it to get it going to his satisfaction, then looked up. 'There's been a series of bank robberies about fifty miles east of here. So far, no one knows who these men are or what they look like and they always strike without warning.'

'Bank robberies, Major?' Steve shook his head in puzzlement. 'Surely the job of running these outlaws to earth is with the law in these towns, the local sheriffs and state marshals. Why does the army come into it?'

Anderson leaned back and spoke through the blue smoke that wreathed his face. 'Two days ago they attacked one of our trains. It was carrying gold bound for the fort. Not only did they get away with all the gold but they also killed fifteen of my best men. Unfortunately, I can't spare any men from the fort. I need someone who knows how these killers operate and from what I've heard you're the best man for the job. Do you know anything of the territory out there?'

Steve pressed his lips into a hard line of concentration. 'That would be close to the north-eastern edge of the Willard Flats, wouldn't it?'

'That's right.'

'But Good God, Major, those flats cover almost half of the state. A man could ride in there and you'd never find him again.'

'I'll admit it won't be easy and it'll be mighty dangerous. If you decline to take the job I'll understand.'

'That isn't the problem, Major. The first thing I'd need to do is find my way around and then try to discover how these outlaws are getting their information.'

'You reckon that where the gold shipment was concerned, they might be getting it from someone here at the fort?'

'It's something to chew over.' Steve paused, then went on, 'Do you know how many men are in this band?'

Anderson knocked the dottle from his pipe and laid it down again. 'All we have at the moment are vague rumours. The numbers range from three to a dozen, depending on who you talk to. My guess is that whenever they need supplies or information, one of them will ride into the nearest town so as not to arouse any suspicion. Going in alone, they'd be just another prospector or cowpoke riding through. They'll never ride in together unless they mean to attack some bank or other. As far as I'm aware there are no wanted posters with their faces on them.'

'Even if there were only three to begin with it's surprisin' how often men join up with outlaws like these. It happened with the James brothers and the Youngers.' Steve switched the subject. 'What's the nearest town to where your train was attacked?'

Anderson got up and walked over to the map on the wall. Without turning his head, he said, 'Fenton. It's just a small place. It's about a day's ride from here if you travel fast. I've met the local sheriff, name of Winton, Jed Winton.'

'Can he be trusted?'

'From what I've seen, I reckon so.'

'Then I guess he's the first man I should see.'

The major came back to his seat. 'Then you'll take the job?'

'Give me a couple o' days to collect everythin' I need and then I'll head out for Fenton.'

'Be careful. These men are clever as well as ruthless. So far, the law's had no success in pinning 'em down and they can smell an undercover law agent a mile away. If there is someone here at the fort passing 'em information, my guess is they'll know by now that you've been here. They'll be on the lookout for any strangers ridin' into Fenton.'

'I guess I'll have to take my chances on that.'

Steve left the major's office, saw to it that his mount was stabled, then walked over to the canteen. It seemed ages since he had last eaten a decent meal. Some of the men there eyed him curiously, noticing the twin Colts in his gunbelt and wondering what this tall dark-haired stranger was doing there. Inside the canteen he ate ravenously. When he'd finished he leaned back in his chair and pushed the empty plate away.

The coffee was hot and strong, burning the back of his throat. He rolled a smoke, lit it and inhaled deeply as he turned over in his mind everything that Major Anderson had told him. Much of this was new country to him. He had heard rumours of the huge wasteland known as the Willard Flats, and what he had been told he didn't particularly like. It certainly seemed to be an ideal place for outlaws to hole up.

Some men in the past had driven their great herds across it to the railroad stations in the north, and doubtless others would continue to do so in the future. But there was danger every step of the way.

By mid-morning of the second day, Steve was ready to ride out of Fort Leveridge. Anderson had asked to see him before he left and it was as he made his way across the parade ground that the gates behind him opened and two riders came in, reining up their mounts a short distance from his.

Steve paused before entering the headquarters and

studied them in sudden surprise. One, he noted, was an Apache. The other was a young woman with long black hair that reached halfway down her back. She wore a straw hat on the back of her head, tied loosely just below her chin. He reckoned she was about twenty-five with a determined look about her that suggested she was used to having her own way. There was also a hint of barely suppressed anger that he couldn't understand.

She did not look at him as he stepped inside, closing the door behind him. Anderson was standing at the window when Steve entered the office. He turned quickly.

'You all ready to ride out, Landers?'

'All set.' Steve affirmed. 'I guess I'll head straight for Fenton and see if I can pick up any information there.'

The major gave a nod of agreement. 'It's possible you may find these people too frightened to talk much to strangers. Jed Winton, the sheriff, might be the best man to see. He'll know most of what's happening around the area.'

'I'll do that, Major, and—' Steve broke off sharply as the door was thrust open and someone came in.

It was the woman he had noticed outside. In the doorway behind her a young soldier stuttered, 'I'm sorry, Major. I told her you were busy but she refused to listen.'

'That's all right, soldier,' Anderson said. 'Return to your post.'

The soldier left, closing the door. To the girl,

Anderson said, 'What is it that seems so urgent you should burst into my office, Miss. . . ?'

'Freya Morgan. My father was the manager of the bank in Fenton until those outlaws rode into town. They shot him in the back when he refused to open the safe. We were promised that the army was here to protect us but so far these killers are allowed to roam the territory unhindered.'

The anger on her features showed through in her voice. The words of her blunt accusation were clipped and she hurled each individual syllable at him like a stone.

Anderson spread his hands in a gesture of resignation. 'Miss Morgan. You can see for yourself how many men I have here under my command and I'm supposed to cover more than a thousand square miles of some of the worst territory in the country.

'It's not up to the army to maintain law and order in Fenton. That's the job of the local sheriff. If events get out of hand, he can always call on the state marshal for help. My job is to maintain peace among the various tribes along the frontier and provide cover for any wagon trains headed this way.'

Freya held her whip tightly in her right hand, tapping it hard against her other gloved hand. 'So you intend doing nothing about it? Not even when one of your own trains was derailed and robbed not far from Fenton and several of your men killed.'

Anderson's head jerked up quickly and there was surprise written all over his lined features. 'What do you know about that train, Miss Morgan? How do you know it was an army train?'

She shrugged. 'Fenton's only a small town and word gets around, Major. But we're straying from the point. The citizens of Fenton are fed up with your promises. These outlaws strike and kill at will.'

'And then seemingly vanish,' Anderson retorted. 'Once they head into the Flats it's almost impossible to hunt them down. However, I understand the feelings of the decent people in your town. I've already arranged for Mr Lander here to ride to Fenton and track down this band.'

The girl swung her glance towards Steve. For an instant, there was a look of derision in her eyes. 'One man against that gang? Are you being serious, Major?'

Without waiting for a reply she turned on Steve and said harshly, 'I mean no disrespect, Mr Landers, but do you expect to run this band to earth on your own?' She shook her head. 'Take it from me, you don't stand a chance and you'll not only find yourself up against the outlaws. There are others who'll be against you. Strangers aren't welcome in Fenton. We also have Hal Clegg running the smaller ranchers off their land and you'll find that his word is law around there, not the sheriff's.'

She swung to face Anderson again, her eyes still blazing with anger. 'And he's another one you've refused to deal with, Major.'

The older man spread his hands in resignation. 'I've made it quite plain, both to you and the other concerned citizens of Fenton, that Hal Clegg is no concern of the army. It's entirely up to the people of

Fenton to stand up to him. So far, I've seen no evidence that Clegg has done anything against the law. Even if he has, you have a sheriff in town and it's up to you to prove these accusations. It's Winton's duty to enforce the law. My job is to patrol the frontier and guard the various trails through this territory.'

'So we're left with one man to solve our problems.' The disdain in her voice cut deeply into Steve.

He forced a grim smile. 'Sometimes, Miss Morgan, one man can slip around unnoticed whereas a posse would be spotted at once.'

'Then I wish you luck. Somehow, I think you'll need it. As for me, it's clear I'll get no satisfaction here. It was simply a waste of my time riding out here but believe me, Major, you haven't heard the last of this.'

Turning on her heel, she stormed out of the office slamming the door behind her.

Anderson sank down into his chair. Quite suddenly he seemed to have aged several years. 'You see how things are, Landers,' he said thinly. 'Everyone expects me to work miracles and do everything with the few resources I have. You know, there are times when I wish I'd never joined the army.'

'I guess I can understand your position, Major.' Steve nodded. 'Before I go, there are a couple more things. Firstly, I reckon you should check every man here who has any knowledge of when your gold shipments are bein' moved. From what you've told me those men must have had prior information about it and some o' that knowledge may have come from here.'

Anderson looked surprised but said, 'I'll do that. And the second thing?'

'This man Clegg whom Miss Morgan mentioned. From what she said it would seem he has some kind o' hold over the town.'

'She may be right. I know very little about the man. Certainly he has the biggest spread in this neck o' the woods and I also understand he owns the bank and also a couple of saloons. But there's no law against that.'

'No, I guess not. But is there any evidence that he might be in cahoots with these outlaws?'

Anderson rubbed his forehead and sat back. 'I'll admit that thought has occurred to me. But I reckon we can dismiss it now. It was his bank that was robbed a few weeks ago.'

'I see. Well, I reckon that's all for the moment, Major. I'll keep you in touch with anything that happens.'

They shook hands, then Steve left the office. Outside, he looked around for any sign of the girl and the Indian but there was nothing to be seen of them or their mounts. Either they had decided to remain at the fort for a few days and had gone to stable their horses or were already on their way back to Fenton.

One of the soldiers brought his horse and provisions. Securing the two bags of food, Steve swung into the saddle. In his pocket was a map of the surrounding territory, which the major had provided for him. Once the gates were open he touched spurs to his mount's flanks and rode out.

The sun was now high in the heavens, nearing its zenith. Shadows were small and the heat beat down on his head and shoulders like the inside of an oven. He sat easy in the saddle knowing there was a long way to go before he reached Fenton. Anderson said that a man could cover that distance in a day by riding hard. That, however, was not his intention. He meant to take his time and see what he was riding into. Ahead of him, where the trail stretched away into the distance, the horizon was clear. Evidently, he mused, Freya Morgan and her companion had remained at the fort.

By mid-afternoon the trail led him into rough country almost completely devoid of vegetation. The blistering heat that had ridden with him since setting out from Fort Leveridge was still hanging in the unmoving air. It soaked through his shirt and brought the sweat out over his entire body. He had crossed several small creeks but these were now simply narrow depressions in the hard-baked earth.

There had obviously been a drought here for several years. On the odd occasion when the rains came these streams would be full of rushing, clear water. Now they were nothing more than minor irregularities on the surface of the land.

Shading his eyes against the stabbing glare of the sun, he scanned the region all around him, then stiffened as something caught his eye. Details wavered and flowed in the heat-laden air and several moments fled before he recognized what it was. A covered wagon and two horses. Touching spurs to the sorrel's flanks, he rode towards it.

Two men stood beside the wagon, one of them appeared to be little more than a boy. Steve immediately noticed where the two nearer wheels had sunk up to their axles in the soft earth. The older man swung round sharply on hearing his approach and reached for the Winchester lying on the buckboard.

Holding his hands high, well clear of the guns at his waist, Steve called, 'You don't need that, friend. I don't aim to rob you.'

The man looked at him with narrowed eyes for a moment, then slowly lowered the rifle. 'Can't be too careful these days,' he said. 'Clegg has sworn to run us clear out o' the territory. I figured you were one o' his killers.'

Steve swung himself from the saddle, threw a quick glance at a woman seated on the buckboard, the reins gripped tightly in her hands. 'You runnin' away from something?' he enquired.

'Ain't it obvious?' grunted the man grimly. 'I'm Seth Warton. These are my wife, Sarah, my son Tom, and there are two more children in the back.' He jerked a thumb towards the rear of the wagon. 'The bank – and that means Clegg – foreclosed on our loan a couple o' weeks ago. We were given that long to get our things together and leave. He took everythin' we had. He said that if we were caught within fifty miles o' town by sundown tonight he'd finish us for good.'

'Then I figure the first thing to do is free this wagon and get it back on the trail.' Steve looked around and spotted the stunted bushes growing alongside the trail a few yards away. 'Help me pull up those bushes and then place them in front o' the wheels,' he ordered crisply.

Within a few minutes the ragged bushes were in place and Steve ordered the man and boy to place their shoulders against the side of the wagon. Calling out to the woman, he said, 'When I give the word give those horses some whip. It's the only way we're goin' to get you out o' this mess.'

To the other two, he said harshly, 'All right, try to push the wagon upright while I give it a heave from the back.'

Getting a firm grip on the ground with his feet, Steve called, 'Now!' Thrusting with all of his strength, he felt the wagon give a little. 'Push harder,' he yelled as the two horses strained forward. At first he thought they were not going to make it. Then with a sudden lurch, the wheels caught on the branches and the wagon rolled forward.

Once it was on firmer ground the woman hauled hard on the reins, bringing the wagon to a standstill. Wiping the sweat from his forehead, Steve straightened up. To Warton he said, 'Reckon you'll be all right now, friend.'

The boy climbed up beside his mother. At the same time Warton cast a worried glance along the trail, narrowing down his eyes. 'We're not out o' danger yet,' he grunted. 'Unless I miss my guess that dust yonder means there are riders coming – and coming fast.'

Steve swung round and made out the white cloud in the distance. From the size of it he reckoned there were about half a dozen men there, spurring their mounts along the trail.

'You know who those riders are?' he asked.

Warton forced a grim smile. 'I don't have to see 'em to know they're Clegg's men. You'd better make yourself scarce, mister. This is our fight, although I reckon the odds are stacked against us.'

Steve's smile was equally grim. 'I don't like the idea o' runnin' when folk are in danger. From what I've heard, this *hombre* Clegg ought to be taught a lesson.'

There was no time in which to say anything more. Warton reached behind him and took down the Winchester, holding it tightly in both hands. The riders swept closer and Steve saw there were five of them, led by a thin man with the sign of the gunfighter written all over him. They skidded to a halt a few feet away, the leader remaining in the saddle. The other four dismounted, spreading out as they edged forward.

The leader stared across at Warton, a leering grin on his sallow features. 'I thought that Mr Clegg told you to be out o' this state afore sundown.' He deliberately lifted his head to measure the position of the sun. 'It don't look to me as though you're goin' to make it. I reckon we'd better finish you here. It'll save us having to ride back all this way after dark.'

Standing with his hands hanging loosely by his sides, Steve said softly, 'Seems to me you like killin' ordinary folk, together with women and children.'

The gunhawk jerked upright in the saddle, his eyes narrowed to mere slits, his features flushed an angry red.

'You aimin' to stop us, *amigo*?' He bared his lips, showing tobacco-stained teeth. 'Or maybe you think you can take on all five of us?'

'Maybe,' Steve said thinly.

The other's grin widened. He turned his head slowly as if to look back at the men behind him. It was a feint but Steve had seen this move several times before. Swiftly, the killer's right hand dropped downward for his gun. It was just clear of the holster when the Colt, which seemed to have leapt miraculously into Steve's hand, spat muzzle flame.

The rider jerked in the saddle. His gun fell from his nerveless fingers before he toppled sideways and hit the ground. For the tiniest fraction of a second he knew what had happened. His body twitched once and then he lay still, his eyes wide and staring but seeing nothing.

Steve turned swiftly, covering the others. Too late, he realized that one of them had moved out of sight. A moment later, the woman seated on the buckboard screamed.

Glancing round, Steve saw that the fifth man had somehow climbed over the back of the wagon. He was now crouched just behind the woman, the muzzle of his revolver pressed hard against the back of her neck, his finger tight on the trigger.

'Now drop your weapons, both of you,' he snarled, 'Or I squeeze this trigger and she dies.'

Inwardly, Steve cursed himself for not keeping an eye on all of the men. He should have anticipated something like this. There was nothing he could do but obey. He allowed the Colt to drop from his hand on to the ground at his feet. Slowly, Warton lowered the Winchester.

'That's better.' The gunhawk stood up, his weapon trained on the woman's head. 'Now move away, both of you.'

Gritting his teeth, Steve did as he was told. He knew that if he made any attempt to go for his other gun, the gunhawk would carry out his threat. He stood with his hands lifted while a riot of thoughts chased each other through his mind.

The gunshot, when it came a few seconds later, made him flinch. He stared at the wagon, expecting to see the woman slumped on the buckboard. Through unbelieving eyes he saw the Colt fall from the gunhawk's hand and land with a clatter on the boards. The killer toppled sideways, crashing on to the dirt beside the wagon.

Still not knowing what had happened, Steve made a dive for his gun. He expected to feel the impact of a bullet before he could reach it, knowing that the rest of Clegg's men still had their weapons, but in that moment, a clear ringing voice called, 'The rest of you drop your guns, very slowly. The first man who tries anything I don't like will join your partner.'

Lifting his head, Steve looked round. Freya Morgan sat her mount a few yards away, a smoking Colt in her right hand covering the three men beside the wagon. At her side was the Indian, his features impassive. There was a rifle in his hands, also trained on the killers.

Steve picked up his Colt and the Winchester, handing the rifle to Warton. 'I guess you saved our lives, Miss Morgan,' he said. 'When I didn't see you on the trail, I figured you'd stayed behind at the fort.'

Freya's lips curved into a cool smile. 'Then it was fortunate for you we decided to leave shortly after you did.' She dismounted and walked forward, her glance on the three men. 'The question now is: what do we do with these three? There's no point in taking them into Fenton. Clegg will have them out of jail within half an hour.'

The Indian spoke for the first time. 'Kill them,' he said dispassionately. 'If you let them go, they cause more trouble for everyone.'

Steve shook his head. 'Much as I agree with you, I don't go with shootin' down anyone in cold blood. I say we keep their guns and send 'em back to Fenton. My guess is that Clegg won't be too pleased with what's happened. He seems the kind o' man who doesn't like failure on the part of his hirelings.'

He turned to the man standing at his side. 'As for you, Mr Warton, your best course would be to ride on. I don't think these men are goin' to bother you now. Keep to the trail and you should reach the safety o' Fort Leveridge before dark.'

Warton nodded. To Freya, he said, 'I can't thank you enough, miss. You saved my wife's life.'

He clambered on to the buckboard and took the reins from his wife's hands. Flicking the whip over the horses' backs, he sent the wagon rolling along the trail.

Steve watched it until it vanished round a bend in the trail, then he turned towards the girl. 'You'll be ridin' on to Fenton, I guess?'

She nodded. 'We should reach there shortly after dark.' Noticing the look of concern on his face, she added, 'You needn't worry on my account. Red Cloud and I can take care of ourselves.'

'And these three?'

She pursed her lips for a moment, then said harshly, 'Let them go but without their guns. We'll take those and throw them away where they'll never find them.' Addressing the trio of gunslingers, she said coldly, 'Get on your mounts and ride.'

The men did as they were told, sullen expressions on their faces as they climbed into the saddle and rode back along the trail towards Fenton. Turning to Steve, she said, 'You're welcome to ride with us, Mr Landers.'

Steve considered her proposal, then shook his head. 'I reckon I'll take my time and hunker down someplace for the night. It's possible we may meet up again sometime.'

'Suit yourself.' She got back into the saddle, wheeled her mount and rode off with the Indian close behind her.

She was a very hard woman, he mused as he watched the dust cloud diminish in the distance. Perhaps it was the manner in which her father had been murdered that had made her this way. The almost off-hand way she had shot that gunman was an indication that she was not a woman to be trifled with;

she was one who went through with everything to which she put her mind.

He buried the bodies of the two gunslingers in the soft earth before leaving. Overhead, the buzzards were already circling, sensing the presence of death.

By evening, with the darkness drawing in from the east, he reckoned he had covered the best part of thirty miles; he decided to rest up for the night. The terrain all around him was mostly rough scrubland but a little way to his right a stand of trees covered the top of a high knoll.

Turning his mount, he headed towards them. Very soon he came upon a narrow trail, little more than a game track that led deep into the trees. Putting his mount to it, he pushed on, lowering his head against the low branches that hemmed in the track on both sides.

He had only gone fifty yards when he reined up swiftly. A flickering orange glow showed out the tall trunks in front of him. He had not anticipated meeting anyone and instinct made him wary. Dismounting without a sound, he edged forward on foot, easing the Colts in their holsters. Through the ring of trees he made out the fire blazing in the middle of a small clearing.

A solitary man sat outlined against the flames. The smell of frying bacon reached Steve a moment later. On the far side of the clearing, a horse stood quietly. Then it snickered softly as it somehow sensed his presence. Stepping forward, he said softly, 'Don't make a move for that rifle beside you, friend. I don't mean you any harm.'

He saw the man jerk and then turn his head swiftly. By the light of the flickering flames, Steve saw that he was an old man with white hair and a lined, grizzled face.

'I ain't got anythin' worth stealing, stranger,' the other muttered as Steve moved closer so that the man could see him.

'I don't want anythin',' Steve replied. 'I'm no outlaw. I'm headin' for Fenton on a job for the army at Fort Leveridge.'

The old man's eyes narrowed a shade as he looked Steve up and down, then he nodded. 'I guess you don't look like one o' these outlaws, mister. But you sure ain't walkin' all the way to Fenton. Where's your mount?'

'Back in the trees yonder,' Steve replied, jerking his thumb behind him. 'I didn't expect to find anyone here. Sorry I startled you, but you can't take any chances these days.'

He whistled up his mount and tethered it to a nearby branch before squatting down close to the fire. 'You got any o' that grub to spare?'

'Sure. I've got plenty.' The old man got to his feet, wincing a little as though his legs pained him. He went across the clearing and brought more food from his saddle-bag. He tossed more bacon into the pan. Sinking back, he said, 'You say you're workin' for the army, mister?'

Steve nodded. 'That's right, old-timer. The name's Landers. I guess you've heard about the train that was attacked and robbed just outside o' Fenton a few days back.'

The other shook his head. 'I don't hear much out here in the wilderness,' he replied. 'My name's Will Corday. Many years ago I used to work for the pony express but my route was way to the north o' here, though I did hear they had an express route that crossed the Willard Flats at some point. But things are changin' now, especially since the war ended. Now they have trains to move the mail around the country.'

He slid a couple of rashers of bacon on to a tin plate, spooned a heap of beans beside them, and handed it to Steve. 'If you've just ridden from Leveridge, I guess you'll be ready for that.'

'Thanks, Will.' While Steve ate, the other brought more wood and placed it on the fire. 'Nights get mighty cold out here,' he said. 'When you git old, you feel it. It works its way into your bones. Tell you the truth, I'm glad you found me. I don't often have any company and a man sometimes gets lonely with no one to talk to. But you say you're headin' for Fenton?'

'That's right. Do you know anythin' about the town?'

'Sure.' Corday gave a jerky nod. 'I suppose it's no better and no worse than a dozen other frontier towns. There's some kind o' law and order there but not much. The sheriff does what he can but so far he's not managed to track down this outlaw band that have been robbin' the banks in this territory. Folk have been talkin' of putting him out of office and replacin' him with a younger man. The trouble with that is that it'll most likely be one o' Clegg's men they elect.'

'And where do you reckon these outlaws have their hideout?'

'Hell, mister, there's only one place they can hide out around these parts – somewhere in the Flats. But that region is so big and dangerous they could be anywhere within fifty or sixty miles.'

'That's the way it looks to me,' Steve agreed. He handed back his empty plate. 'Do you happen to know if the sheriff ever got a posse together and went in there after this band?'

Corday rubbed his chin. It made a faint scratching sound in the silence. 'I did hear once that he sent five men out to hunt these critters down but the talk was that none o' them came back. My guess is they either caught up with 'em and got killed, or they figgered the Flats are too dangerous to move around in 'em and they just kept on ridin'.'

Steve pondered on that for a moment, then shrugged. 'There's one other thing.' He rolled himself a smoke, placed it between his lips and lit it, blowing the smoke into the air. 'How much do you know o' this man, Clegg?'

'Hal Clegg? Everyone knows him. He runs this territory.' The note of the old man's voice changed abruptly as he asked, 'He ain't wanted by the army, is he?'

'Now why do you ask that?'

Corda shrugged. 'Just a feelin' I've got. He ain't got to be where he is now without bein' involved in some illegal deals. You can take my word for that.'

'I'm sure you're right. On my way here I ran into a small family drivin' a wagon. They told me that this man Clegg had driven 'em off their ranch and if they weren't over the border by sundown, he'd send his men after 'em.'

Corday hunched himself a little closer to the fire and pulled up the high collar of his jacket. 'That's the sort o' thing he would do,' he acknowledged soberly. 'What happened?'

'Five of his men turned up and threatened to kill 'em. I shot their leader and when another had the drop on this fella's wife, Freya Morgan shot him.'

Corday uttered a cackling laugh. 'That's the sort o' thing I'd expect of her. She's her father's daughter all right. Afraid o' nobody.' He sobered instantly and a worried frown crossed his grizzled features. 'But Clegg won't let that go. Someone will have to pay for killin' two of his men. I'd watch your back if you ride into Fenton. And try to keep an eye on Freya if you can. She's been too outspoken against Clegg after her father was shot, accusin' him of being behind her father's murder.'

'I will,' Steve promised. He got up. 'Well, thanks for the grub. I guess I'll turn in. I've got a long ride tomorrow.'

Steve took his bedroll, spread it out near the fire and stretched himself out on it. The pleasant warmth from the fire suffused his entire body as he stared up at the trees above him. The last thing he saw before he fell asleep was the old man squatting beside the fire, his lined face a red blur in the firelight.

*

When Steve woke it was to find the grey dawn light filtering through the branches. The fire was still blazing and he guessed that the old man had scarcely slept at all through the night. There was the smell of bacon frying.

While they ate Corday said, 'You wouldn't be lookin' for company on the way to Fenton, would you? I may be an old man but I won't hold you up and if we should meet with these outlaws, I can still use this Winchester.'

Steve thought over the other's proposal. He hadn't counted on meeting up with anyone after the encounter of the afternoon, but there was the fact that Corday asserted that he was familiar with Fenton to be taken into consideration. It was possible he might learn something important on the way. 'Sure, you can come along, old-timer,' he said after a reflective pause. 'Be glad o' your company.'

Less than an hour later they rode out of the trees into the blazing sunlight. The trail Corday chose took them in a wide arc, skirting around the southern arm of the Flats. Here the land was harsh and glaring in the brilliant sunlight. Little grew in the barren soil apart from clumps of mesquite and spiny cactus.

'It looks the ideal place for anyone wanting to hide from the law, don't it?' Corday said, inclining his head in the direction of the wasteland.

Nodding in agreement, Steve asked, 'You said you once worked with the pony express in the old days.

Were there any places yonder where men might hide out?'

Corday pursed his lips into a thin line of concentration. 'Now you come to mention it, I guess there must've been, but that was way out o' my territory. If they did have a route across these Flats, they'd have set up at least a couple o' changing stations where the riders got fresh horses and somethin' to eat.

'But the way I heard it they then decided that the Flats weren't the best o' places to keep way stations. What with the blisterin' heat and the terrain, they pulled 'em out and left the stations to fall into disuse and decay. They found a longer trail to the north. That were the one I used to ride.

'But at times the big herds o' cattle would come this way from Texas to places like Benson and Bitter Creek – but they never stayed in that hellhole long enough to build anythin' like a town. I guess places like the Flats are a sore on the face o' the earth. No one can scrape a livin' out o' that parched ground. To me it's like a place God decided to make and then decided to leave half-finished.'

'I guess so,' Steve agreed. 'But it wouldn't have to be a town to hide a handful o' men.'

'Nope. I guess not. Any place would do so long as it provided shelter and was hidden away from pryin' eyes. They'd also have another advantage.'

Steve glanced at the other in surprise. 'What would that be?' he enquired.

Corday gave a toothy grin. 'If you'd ever been in

there, you'd know. There are times when the wind gets up blowing that dust and alkali for miles across the territory. Within minutes it can totally obliterate any tracks.'

'So if anyone did follow this gang they'd soon lose 'em.'

'That the way of it,' Corday agreed solemnly.

'No doubt these outlaws were well aware of that if they chose this place as a hideout,' Steve remarked grimly.

They rode on in silence for almost an hour before they came upon a narrow river that ran directly across their trail. Here they allowed their mounts to drink and rest. The glaring sunlight now struck hard on their heads and shoulders. Where the wastelands stretched away to their left, the entire land shimmered as if covered by a layer of water.

Squatting in the shade of a juniper, Steve asked, 'How much further to Fenton?'

'I reckon we should reach the town before sundown,' Corday replied, chewing on a wad of tobacco. 'Fenton ain't as bad as most o' the frontier towns but sometimes it ain't easy to keep law and order.'

'Anyone I should watch out for?'

Corday sat in silence for a while before answering. 'You know about Clegg. Reckon it'd be best to keep on the right side o' him. At least until you know a bit more about what's goin' on.'

'Just what kind o' man is he?'

Corday spat the wad of tobacco on to the ground.

'He's the banker in Fenton and the biggest landowner around these parts. As well as the bank he owns most o' the property, a couple o' saloons and the hotel. Most o' the folk there have loans from him and if he doesn't particularly like anyone he just forecloses on 'em and takes over their land and house.'

'I guess he must have plenty of enemies in town.'

Corday grinned. 'That don't bother him none. He has plenty o' men on his payroll to make sure no one makes any trouble where he's concerned. They either pull up stakes and leave – or they end up on Boot Hill.'

'Thanks for the warnin', old-timer. I'll keep an eye open for him.'

'Reckon you'd better. He's not the kind o' man I'd like to cross.'

As another thought struck him, Steve asked, 'Do you reckon there might be a tie-in between this man Clegg and these outlaws?'

Corday's brow furrowed in thought. 'Can't see one. His own bank was hit a few days ago by those critters. It ain't likely he'd be in with 'em.'

By early evening they came across a broad well-beaten trail that angled sharply towards the north. Here the going was easier and they let their mounts pick their own pace. The territory now provided a welcome change from the Flats. Tree-covered slopes showed in the distance to their right.

A couple of miles further on the trail dipped into a wide arroyo, which extended for perhaps half a mile. Coming out of it, Steve saw, in the distance, a dark smudge on the horizon.

Pointing, Corday said harshly, 'There's Fenton. Like I said, it ain't a bad town but now and again trouble flares between the ranchers. When that happens, if you're on the wrong side, things can get real bad for you.'

'I don't aim to take sides in any cattle feud,' Steve said sharply. 'I've got a job to do. Once that's finished I aim to ride out.'

'Sometimes a man can't help bein' drawn into trouble,' his companion commented. 'It can come on you when you ain't looking.'

The sun had gone down before they rode into Fenton and lights were beginning to show in the saloons. The town had been built on either side of a narrow river and there was a board-bridge spanning the rushing water. Steve ran his gaze over it as he reined up his mount at the end of the street on the western bank.

Even at first sight Fenton was unlike any other frontier town he'd seen. The houses on the eastern bank of the river were large and clearly belonged to people with money. The western bank was the commercial side of the town, any dwellings being much less grand than the others.

'Strange how they built this place, ain't it?' Corday remarked laconically in answer to Steve's questioning look. 'But my guess is there's a reason for it.'

'And what might that be?' Steve asked.

In answer, the other pointed towards the far side of the river. 'The big grasslands are all to the north and east. Those large houses you see yonder belong to the big cattlemen and folk like Hal Clegg. The rest o' the townsfolk live on this side o' the river.'

Steve nodded. 'And that bridge sits right between them.' He eyed it speculatively. It was almost as if the bridge represented the dividing line between the rich and the not so rich in this town.

Turning his head he spotted the sheriff's office a short distance away. He rode towards it. 'Guess I'd better make myself known to the law here,' he said in answer to Corday's enquiring look. He looped the reins around the hitching rail and stepped up on to the boardwalk. he knocked twice on the door, then went inside.

The man sitting behind the desk was grey-haired and now running to fat. He glanced up sharply, brows drawn together, as Steve entered.

'I guess you're Sheriff Winton,' Steve said. 'Mind if I sit down?'

'Help yourself, mister.' Winton indicated the chair in front of his desk. 'What brings you to Fenton?'

'Well now, Sheriff. I figure you might have already received word from Fort Leveridge about me. The name's Landers, Steve Landers. I'm here about these robberies in this part o' the territory but more particularly about the theft o' that gold from the army train.'

Winton got to his feet and extended a hand. 'I'm mighty glad you're here, Landers,' he said affably. 'Believe me, I could do with your help.' He opened the drawer of his desk and took out a bottle and a couple of glasses. He poured out a drink and pushed it across to Steve.

A moment later the street door opened again and Corday came in. For a moment there was an expression of surprise on the lawman's face.

'This is a friend o' mine,' Steve explained. 'I met him on the ride here.'

The sheriff's lips twisted into a faint smile. 'I'm well acquainted with Will,' he said drily. 'He's spent the night in my jail on several occasions – drunk and shootin' at anything with that old Winchester of his. He might've killed someone, or got himself killed. I had to do it for his own good.'

'I'll keep an eye on him,' Steve promised. 'It's possible he might be useful to me. He reckons he knows his way around Fenton and he can keep his eyes open for any strangers who might ride in.'

Winton leaned forward over the desk. Lowering his voice, he asked, 'You reckon there might be somebody in town who's helping these outlaws?'

'The thought had occurred to me, Sheriff. Likewise, I figure somebody back at Fort Leveridge is passing information to them. Major Anderson is checking on that. If he finds anything definite he'll get word to me.'

Winton scratched his chin. 'You seem to have all o' your trails covered, Landers. If there's any way I can be of help, just ask.'

'There is. I noticed one odd fact about the town as I rode in. It seemed to me that the river not only divides Fenton into two halves but also the folk who live here.'

Winton leaned forward on his elbows and placed the tips of his fingers together. 'You're right, Landers. The saloons and hotels are all on this side, where the drifters and those you'd call the lower class live. All those who have money live in the big houses on the other side.'

'Is that how it's always been?'

'I guess so. At least as far back as I can recall. There's very little mixin' of the two.'

Steve pushed back his chair and got to his feet. After a pause he said, 'Just one more thing, Sheriff. I reckon you get to know quite a lot o' what goes on in town. Could these outlaws have any connection with this guy Hal Clegg I've been hearin' about?'

'Clegg?' A gust of surprise flashed across the lawman's weathered features. 'What makes you ask that? Those varmints robbed his bank a few days ago. Shot the manager in the back and made off with a heap o' money and gold. You're not suggestin' he was in on that robbery, are you?'

Steve shrugged. 'I look at every possibility, Sheriff. Men have been known to do just that, especially if they insure the bank against robbery with one o' these big businesses back East. That way, they get their money back and also take a cut from the outlaws.'

Winton had clearly not considered that possibility. He scratched his chin, then said, 'Well, Landers, I wish you luck. With this band o' killers on the loose I reckon you're goin' to need it.'

Outside on the boardwalk, Steve said, 'I guess I'd better get somethin' to eat and then find myself a place to stay.'

The oldster pointed across the street. 'Yonder's the best place. You can get a bed and the food there is the best in town. I should warn you, however, it's one o' Clegg's establishments. He may not take it too kindly if he knows who you are.'

'Thanks for the warnin'. Are you comin' too?'

Corday shook his head. 'That place ain't for the likes o' me, *amigo.* The groom at the end o' the street is a good friend o' mine. I've got a place there in the stables whenever I'm in town. I'll take your mount and get him fed and stabled for you.'

After the old man had gone Steve made his way across the street. He had just stepped up on to the opposite boardwalk when a voice called, 'Mr Landers.'

Turning swiftly, he saw that two riders were reining up their mounts a few feet away. Freya Morgan sat her horse easily, and was surveying him with a cool, appraising gaze.

Leaning against the hitching rail, he said calmly, 'Have you just arrived back in town, Miss Morgan?'

'No. We got back late this morning after riding all night. I see you've already met one of our local characters. The trouble with Will Corday is that he talks too much. One of these days that's going to be the end of him.' She dismounted lightly and she handed the reins to the Indian accompanying her. 'Take the horses to the stables, Red Cloud,' she commanded. 'I have to talk to our friend here.'

'I was just about to get something to eat,' Steve told her. 'I arrived only a few minutes ago. Would you join me? We can talk while we eat.'

He saw her hesitate but it was only momentarily. Nodding, she fell into step beside him as he entered the small hotel. Once seated at the table near the window, Steve said evenly, 'I know you probably don't like me and you've got it in your head that one man won't be able to bring these killers to justice.

'But this isn't the first case like this I've handled. I've come up against these outlaw gangs before. Besides, my first job is to discover where they're holed up.'

'And do you have any ideas about that?' Freya asked.

'Some. Wherever their hideout is, it can't be too far from Fenton.'

'How do you know that?' Freya paused with her fork halfway to her mouth. She looked surprised.

Steve grinned. 'I'd say that's pretty obvious. The gold shipment they took from that train was quite heavy. Unless they had spare horses – which I doubt – it would be mighty difficult to carry it any distance.'

'That makes sense, I suppose. But there are still plenty of places around here where they could hide. Sheriff Winton thinks they're up in the hills somewhere.'

'You talked to the sheriff?'

'Of course. You know from what you heard back at Fort Leveridge that they killed my father when he refused to open the bank safe for them. They never gave him a chance to defend himself. It was cold-blooded murder.'

Steve thought he saw tears in her eyes but she dashed them away with the back of her hand. He said softly, 'And you want revenge. That's only natural, I reckon.'

'I want to see them brought in and hanged from the nearest tree.' The bitter anger inside her showed through in her voice. Her face hardened abruptly. Quite suddenly, in the space of a few moments, she appeared to be a totally different woman.

Steve pushed away his empty plate. He rolled himself a smoke and sat back in his chair. 'Tell me,' he said, 'how much do you know about Clegg? I gather he's quite a big man where this town is concerned.'

'Hal Clegg! Believe me the less you have to do with him, the better. What would you want with him? Surely you don't think he's in with these outlaws?'

With a shrug, Steve lit the cigarette. 'Let's just say I always like to know as much as possible about everyone of importance. Clegg seems to be the one who owns quite a bit o' Fenton. My experience is that a man doesn't get to a position like that without havin' a hand in somethin' unlawful.'

He saw the girl hesitate. He could guess what she was thinking. It wasn't wise to talk about this man while you were in Fenton.

She glanced quickly around the small room, then said in a low voice, 'Clegg came to Fenton some twelve years ago from someplace back East. There was talk that he made his money selling arms and information to the Confederate Army. Whether that's true or not, I don't know. But he wasn't here long before he began buying up as much land as he could.'

'I see. If it is true it just confirms my suspicions that he's a man with no scruples, who gets what he wants by any means at his disposal. Where's his place?'

'It's about two miles out of town to the north. Almost all of the land there belongs to him. There were one or two ranchers who had spreads there but they all pulled out shortly after Clegg arrived.'

'I'll bet they did. I've seen it all before nearly everywhere along the frontier. The smaller ranchers are forced to sell or they leave at the point of a gun.'

Once their meal was finished, Steve accompanied her to the door. 'You've been very helpful, Miss Morgan. You're sure you'll get home all right?'

'Don't worry. I'll be quite safe. Besides, Red Cloud is waiting for me.' She uttered a low laugh as Steve glanced around. 'You won't see him but he's in the shadows over there.' She pointed across the street and a moment later, the Indian emerged from the darkness and stood waiting for her.

As she moved away, she said, 'If you want any more information, I suggest you have a talk with Ed Casson.'

'Who's he?'

'He owns the local newspaper. I guess he knows most of what goes on in Fenton.'

Steve watched her walk towards the waiting Indian. As he turned to go back into the hotel, he wondered just who this Red Cloud was and how he came to be associated with Freya Morgan.

He had almost reached the door when the sound of riders approaching drew his attention back to the street. There were three of them. Steve eyed them closely as they drew level with him, pulling their mounts to a halt. Two of the men were obviously gunfighters. Steve recognized their type at once: hired killers who thought nothing of shooting a man in the back or from the shadows.

The third was shorter than either of the others, running to fat. His clothing was clearly of the best, tailored somewhere back East. A diamond pin showed off his white cravat.

'You just ridden into town, stranger?' he demanded.

'That's right.' Steve nodded. 'But I don't see that's any business o' yours.'

'Everythin' that goes on in Fenton is my business.'

The fat man leaned forward over the pommel. 'I'm Hal Clegg. This is my town and I don't like strangers wanderin' around unless I know why they're here.'

'It seems to me you take quite a lot on yourself, Mr Clegg. So who gave you the right to own everyone in this town?'

Clegg gave a sneering smile. 'Men like these two at my back. They're paid to do whatever I say. Anyone who doesn't agree with that can either ride out or be carried out to Boot Hill.'

Steve said nothing but stood with his eyes drilling into Clegg's. He was, however, watching the two riders behind him. It was plain that both men were itching to go for their guns the moment Clegg gave the order.

After some moments Steve said thinly, 'I've met a lot o' men like you, Clegg; men who force their will on others. I wonder just how many you've had killed just to get where you are now?'

Somehow, Clegg was holding his obvious anger in control but there was a ruddy flush on his coarse features as he retorted, 'I also figure you're the gunslick who killed one o' my men along the trail a piece this afternoon.'

He eyed Steve up and down, his small eyes taking in every detail. 'You seem to be a man handy with a gun. My guess is you're a loner, moving from town to town and never stayin' long in the same place. However, I'm willin' to overlook what happened on the trail if you work for me. I need good men I can trust and—'

'Save your breath, Clegg. I don't work for the likes o' you. My business here is my own, and when it's finished I'll ride out again.'

Clegg flushed and his face twisted into angry lines. 'If you cross me, mister, you'll never live to ride out o' town. I've offered you a fair deal. Refuse it and you'll wish you'd never seen Fenton.'

Steve lowered his right hand until it was close beside the Colt at his side. 'I suggest you ride on, Clegg, before you say somethin' you're likely to regret. I reckon I've already made my position clear.'

For a moment, Steve thought the two men with Clegg intended to go for their guns but a sharp word from Clegg stopped them. 'We'll leave this man for the time bein'. He's in town for some reason and when I find out what it is, I'll deal with him. I know where to find him the next time. Just think things over carefully, mister. As I've just told you, this is my town.

Remember that if you want to stay healthy. I'm the law here. I give the orders, not your friend Winton, as you'll soon discover to your cost.'

Jerking savagely on the bridle, he swung his mount around and rode back along the street with his two gunmen trailing after him. Steve watched him go, then went back into the hotel, closing the door behind him.

3

THE BACK-SHOOTERS

Will Iliff was standing at the door of the run-down saloon at Mender's Crossing, swatting angrily at the horde of flies that swarmed around the old building. That last robbery they had carried out had been a success but he still felt angry and frustrated at being cooped up in this hellhole of a place. As far as he was concerned there was enough money and gold from that army shipment to keep all of them in luxury for the rest of their days.

A few moments later Minter came out and joined him, taking off his hat and wiping his forehead with the back of his hand. It was almost high noon and the heat was suffocating.

'No sign of him yet?' he demanded harshly.

'Nope.' Iliff shook his head. 'He's been gone for more than three hours. He should be back by now unless somethin's happened in town. I told you I should have gone instead.'

'Butler knows exactly what to do,' Minter retorted. He shaded his eyes against the stabbing glare of the sun and peered off towards the south-east. 'Besides, there ain't any Wanted notices posted with our faces on 'em so nobody will recognize him.'

'Maybe not. It ain't the townsfolk I'm worried about. But I never did like goin' in with this *hombre* Clegg.'

Minter swung on him. 'We work with Clegg because we need him,' he growled. 'He claims he knows where we're holed up and I can't take the chance that he's just bluffin'. If he's tellin' the truth, one word from him to the army and we're finished.'

Iliff spat into the dirt. 'So he just sits there on his big ranch, doing nothin', while we take all the risks and then hand over a quarter of what we get.'

'I don't like the idea any more than you do, but that's the way it is. Besides, we've got gold bars in there.' He jerked a thumb behind him towards the saloon door. 'It's no use to us as it is. We need somebody like Clegg to get it changed into dollar bills.' He caught Iliff's arm and pointed. 'Here comes Jim now.'

Five minutes later Butler reined up his mount in the middle of the dusty street and slid wearily from the saddle. Leading the horse towards the wooden post he tied the reins to it, then stepped up on to the creaking boardwalk.

'Well?' Minter demanded roughly. 'What did Clegg say?'

'Let me get a drink first,' Butler rasped. 'It's as hot as the hinges o' hell out there. My throat's as dry as the inside of an oven.'

He brushed past the two men and entered the saloon. Taking the top off a bottle, he drank it down while Minter waited with ill-concealed impatience.

'All right, Jim.' He spat the words out. 'Did you see Clegg and give him our proposition?'

'I saw him all right.' Butler threw the empty bottle through the open door. It hit the street and shattered. 'But he seems to be gettin' some mighty big ideas of his own. He wants a third share in everythin' we get.'

Minter's face twisted into a scowl. 'We have an agreement with him. It says he gets a quarter. He ain't goin' back on it now.'

Butler shrugged. 'He figures he's got a hold over us. Either we agree or he lets Winton and the army at Fort Leveridge know where we're hidin' out. From the way he said it, I'd say he means it.'

'I said you should have let me go talk with him,' Iliff snarled, showing his tobacco-stained teeth in a vicious grimace. 'Had I been there, he'd have found himself lookin' down the barrel of a gun.'

Minter swung on him. 'That's the way you always do things, Iliff. Make a gun do the talkin' for you. That's why I'm the leader o' this gang and not you. That's why we're still alive today and not buried up in Boot Hill. Shoot down Clegg and we'll have more'n a score o' hired gunmen on our trail. Those men he's got workin' for him are all gunhawks and they won't stop until they get us.'

'So what do you reckon we should do? Give him his third?'

Minter grinned. 'Take it from me, Will, he'll see sense and come round to our way o' thinking once I've had a talk with him. The two o' you stay here. I'm takin' a little ride into town.'

He tossed his cigarette, half-smoked, on to the floor and ground it out under his heel. Outside, the heat was becoming more and more intense. It did little to alleviate the deep-seated anger that boiled inside him, anger directed against Hal Clegg. How the man had discovered their hideout he didn't know. He wasn't even sure that Clegg really did know, but it was a chance he couldn't take. Over the years Clegg had been hiring gunfighters to strengthen his hold on Fenton. If Clegg did know about Mender's Crossing he and his two companions would stand no chance against all of those men.

He rode slowly, keeping his eyes open. Men rarely ventured into this region but there was always the chance of some wagon train hoping to cross it on the way West. By the time Fenton came into sight the sun was well past its zenith but there was still no coolness in the air. He took a narrow trail around the town. Not that he was afraid of being recognized by any of the townsfolk. Most of them already knew him by sight as a fairly regular visitor coming into town for supplies. Since he and the others were never seen together, no one identified them with the outlaw gang that terrorized this part of the territory.

He rode towards Clegg's place from this direction

because the man didn't post lookouts along this part of the perimeter of his land. According to Clegg's way of thinking, if there were to be any trouble it would come from the town. Furthermore, the main part of his herd roamed the rich pastureland to the north of the ranch house and he had plenty of outriders keeping watch on them.

After easing his way through a broad stand of trees, Minter came upon the herd of cattle fifteen minutes later. There was a fire burning in a large hollow and he rode directly towards it. Five men sat in a circle around it, spooning food into their mouths. Two others stood a short distance away. Both held Winchesters.

'All right, mister. Hold it right there,' called one of them harshly.

Reining up, Minter leaned forward and rested his arm across the pommel. 'I'm here to see Hal Clegg,' he said evenly. 'Is he up at the house?'

'Who wants him?' the man demanded.

'Matt Minter. He's met me before. Now – is one o' you goin' to take me to him or do I go there myself?' He saw that the men were undecided.

Then the cowhand with the rifle said, 'I'll get my mount. Then you follow me.'

The man whistled up one of the horses and swung himself into the saddle, still keeping a tight hold on the rifle. He led the way at a brisk pace. Ten minutes later they rode into the wide courtyard fronting the large house. Clegg must have seen them approaching, for he came out to stand on the long veranda just as

Minter slid from the saddle.

Clegg's broad features were grim as he said loudly, 'Somehow, I figured you might come, Minter, after my little talk with your friend this mornin'. If you're hopin' I've changed my mind, you've had a wasted journey.'

Minter's face hardened. Stepping forward, he said tautly, 'I reckon it might be better if we was to talk inside, Clegg. This is a private matter between the two of us.' He threw a meaningful glance in the direction of the cowpoke beside him.

'Suit yourself,' Clegg retorted. 'But there ain't much to talk about unless you're willin' to agree to my terms.'

'Do I take his guns, boss?' interrupted the cowhand.

Minter swung on him. 'Nobody takes my guns,' he snarled menacingly. 'Try it and there'll be a slug in you before you can bring up that rifle.'

The man flushed and for a moment seemed on the point of making his play. Then Clegg said, 'It's all right, Slim. Go back to the others.'

Hesitating, the other sat his mount, glaring at Minter. Then with a muttered oath, he jerked on the reins and rode off. Minter followed Clegg into the house.

Once inside the parlour Clegg said thinly, 'I think I made my position quite clear to your friend. You made quite a haul when you hit that army train carrying all that gold. Now you have the soldiers after you and to me that means that things have changed a lot. Money is one thing, but gold is an entirely different matter.

'That has to be disposed of very carefully, otherwise awkward questions will be asked. You need someone who can be trusted implicitly to buy that gold from you, someone who asks no questions and keeps everything quiet, specially where the army is concerned. Do you know such a person, Minter?'

When the other remained silent, Clegg went on, 'No, I thought not. But I do have the means of turning that gold into dollars and getting you a good return on it. But that person also wants a cut. Hence, I think that a third as my share is a good deal as far as you're concerned.'

'Not a chance. We do all the work, run all o' the risks, and you do nothin'.'

Clegg took a cigar from his vest pocket. He bit off the end before lighting it. Through the smoke, he said smoothly, 'There's always the possibility that the army might get to know exactly where you're hidin' out.'

Minter's face was suddenly suffused with anger. 'Don't make threats, Clegg,' he grated. 'You seem to forget that we only have to talk about the deal we have regarding the robbery on your bank. If these people from back East should learn you were in on it, I doubt if they'll pay you for the money we took. You might find yourself in jail.'

'While you and your companions would be swingin' on the end of a rope,' Clegg warned. 'Think it over, Minter. We both need each other. Besides, there's somethin' else I reckon you ought to know.'

'Oh, and what might that be?'

'A stranger rode into town a couple o' days ago.

He's stayin' at the hotel. He looks like a federal marshal to me.' Clegg shrugged. 'O' course, he might just be some cowpoke lookin' for a job or a loner passin' through on the way West. But I don't think you can afford to take chances. The army won't take the loss of all that gold lyin' down, or the loss of all those men. They'll send somebody to hunt you down and he might just be the one they've sent.'

Clegg took a second cigar from his pocket and handed it to Minter, who took it with a scowl still on his face. 'Just think it over.' Clegg struck a match and lit Minter's cigar. 'You can't keep ridin' into town, otherwise folk might become suspicious. But I can keep a eye on this *hombre* and make sure he doesn't find anythin'.' His lips curled into a faint smile. 'If he should become a nuisance, I can alway arrange for him to be killed.'

Minter blew smoke into the air. 'All right, Clegg,' he said. 'I've thought it over. You keep watch on this stranger and you'll get a third o' the takings.'

'Now you're showin' some sense.' Clegg walked across to the cabinet on the far side of the room and returned with a bottle of whiskey and two glasses. He set them down on the table, poured out two drinks and handed one to Minter.

'We'll drink to our future success,' he said jovially. 'May it long continue.' There was a pause, then Clegg went on, 'I assume that you'll arrange for that gold to be in the usual place for me to pick up.'

Minter gave a terse nod. 'It'll be there tomorrow night,' he said.

He left the ranch and rode back through the town. Inwardly, he was disturbed by the news that a stranger had ridden into Fenton. He had expected it to happen some time. By now the news of their exploits would have travelled across most of the state. The law would be looking for them everywhere. But, unlike the other outlaw gangs across the West, they had one big advantage. No one had ever seen their faces when they carried out their hold-ups. As far as the citizens of Fenton were concerned they were only to be seen individually and, apart from Clegg, no one knew their true identities.

The sun was lowering towards the west by the time he rode into the ghost town of Mender's Crossing. Iliff and Butler were squatting on the boardwalk, smoking. Neither stood up as he lowered himself from the saddle.

'Did you have any more luck than I did?' Butler raised a half-empty bottle to his lips and drained it.

Through thinned lips, Minter muttered, 'Clegg gets the third share he wants.'

'You gave in to him?' Iliff pushed himself upright. 'What the hell are you doin', Matt? The deal was that we all get an equal share.'

Minter leaned his elbows on the hitching rail. It creaked ominously but somehow held his weight. 'Do you think I don't know that?' he muttered thickly. 'But it seems that things have changed. There's a stranger in town, rode in a couple o' days ago. Clegg reckons he's some kind o' marshal.'

'So you figure the law's tryin' to catch up with us at

last?' Iliff queried.

'It could be.' Minter lit a cigarette and inhaled deeply, his brow furrowed. 'It could be dangerous for any of us to ride in and start askin' questions. However, Clegg's offerin' to do that and also keep a close watch on this *hombre.* If he does turn out to be a lawman, Clegg will also make sure he doesn't bother us.'

'How does he intend doin' that?' Butler enquired.

Without turning his head, Minter grunted. 'Accidents can happen – or he gets into a quarrel with some o' Clegg's men and he finishes up on Boot Hill.'

A little more than halfway along the main street Steve pushed open the door of the newspaper office and went in. He picked out the smell of ink right away. A man sat behind a desk on a high stool while another was setting up the press in the middle of the room.

The man at the desk looked up sharply as Steve entered. He was a small, thin-framed man in his late fifties, Steve reckoned, his hair greying around the temples.

'Which of you is Ed Casson? Steve asked.

'I'm Ed Casson,' replied the man at the desk. 'This is Jeb Forrester, my assistant. Do you want to put something in the paper, friend?'

Steve shook his head. 'The name's Landers,' he told the editor. 'Steve Landers. At the moment I'm workin' for Major Anderson at Fort Leveridge.'

Casson gave a brief nod. 'Then I reckon I can guess why you're here, Landers,' he said evenly. 'You're after these danged outlaws that have been plaguing this territory for far too long. It's about time someone did somethin' about it.'

'Then you might be prepared to give me some information. Freya Morgan suggested you'd be the best man to help me.'

'You know Freya?'

'We've met, both here and at Fort Leveridge,' Steve conceded.

'Danged shame about her father.' Forrester spoke without looking up from the press. 'Shot in the back without a chance to defend himself. We published a piece about it in the paper hoping to stir the townsfolk up but we got little response. Seems the folk are too scared to do anythin'.'

'Did Clegg say anythin' about what you wrote?'

'Hal Clegg! Why are you interested in him? I figured you're here because o' these outlaws.'

Steve shrugged. 'I have my reasons. It's just a gut instinct I've got at the moment. That's why I need more information.'

'Nobody knows much about Clegg. He has a big stake in this town. He didn't like what I wrote about him, even threatened to close down the paper.'

'And how do you feel about that?'

'I'm here to give folk the truth as I see it. If Clegg doesn't like it, that's too bad.'

'Is there any evidence that Clegg might be in cahoots with these outlaws?'

Casson, who had been staring out of the dust-smeared window, turned abruptly to face Steve. It was clearly a question he had not expected. He hesitated for a long moment before replying.

'It's mighty strange you should ask that. I've had my suspicions for quite a while but unfortunately Clegg is a very clever man. You can be sure that if there is anything between them, he'll have made sure it's well concealed. The only thing I do know for certain is that Clegg has been regularly receiving quite large sums of money from some source.'

'How did you get hold of that information?'

There was a faint smile on the older man's face as he said, 'An editor always protects the identity of his informants. Let's just say that I know someone who works in the bank.' His gaze returned to the window, and a moment later he went on, 'It would seem to me that someone is very interested in your present whereabouts, Landers. You see that cowpoke standing on the other side of the street. He's been lounging there ever since you came in.'

Steve eyed the man in question. He recognized the type at once. Clearly a Mexican, he had his sombrero pulled down well over his eyes. A cigarette dangled from his lower lip and although he appeared to be looking at nothing in particular, it was obvious he was keeping the office under close surveillance.

'Do you know who he is?'

It was Forrester who answered him. 'Sure. I don't know his name but he's one o' Clegg's hired hands. He's got a reputation as a gunfighter.'

Straightening up, Steve hitched his gunbelt a little higher around his waist. 'I reckon I'd better see what he wants,' he said quietly.

'Be careful,' Forrester warned. 'These men are killers. It's more than likely there'll be another couple waiting somewhere if you make your play with him.'

'I will.' Steve stepped out on to the boardwalk. The Mexican did not move, gave no outward indication that he was even aware of Steve's presence. He knew the type of man he was dealing with. He was the kind who preferred to shoot an opponent in the back rather than face him in fair fight. Turning on his heel, he walked slowly away from the newspaper office.

Next door to it was a gunsmith's shop with a variety of weapons in the window. Steve gave them a seemingly casual glance as he paused. In the window he could make out the reflection of the man opposite. About twenty yards away to his left another gunman was standing at the corner where a narrow alley led away towards the outskirts of town. A quick look passed between the two men, and in the same moment both went for their guns.

The twin Colts seemed to leap into Steve's hands as he twisted and went down on one knee, squeezing the triggers in the same fluid movement. The Mexican jerked as if he'd been slammed in the stomach with a pile-driver. He went backwards on to his heels, crashing against the rails as his spurs caught in the wooden boards. Wood splintered beneath his weight as he fell. The gun in his hand spat muzzle flame, the slug cutting a deep furrow in the dust.

The second man was still standing upright, struggling to keep life in his body. Then he swayed, put out his free hand to clutch at a nearby post. His swarthy features twisted into a spasm of agony. Then the starch went out of him, his knees bent, and he dropped on to his face. His body jerked once, then he lay still.

Steve thrust the Colts back into their holsters, went forward and turned the two bodies over with his foot. Several of the townsfolk were watching and a moment later Casson and Forrester came running over.

'I saw everythin' that happened,' Casson yelled loudly. 'These two men drew first. Like the critters they are they meant to shoot this fella in the back. Just like Morgan was shot in the bank.'

From the corner of his eye Steve saw Winton approaching. The sheriff stared down at the two dead men, then said to Casson. 'You willin' to testify to what I just heard you say?'

'Too danged right I am,' Casson affirmed. 'I reckon it's about time somebody stood up to Clegg and his hired killers.'

'All right.' The sheriff nodded. 'Get them to the morgue.'

Drawing Steve to one side, he muttered in a low voice, 'This could be trouble, Landers. Clegg ain't goin' to be pleased when he hears you've shot down two of his men. I reckon it might be wise if you were to lie low for a while outside o' town somewhere.'

Steve thinned his lips. 'I came here to do a job, Sheriff, and I aim to do it.'

'Sure, sure. I understand that. But pretty soon Clegg will come ridin' into town and you can't fight all o' his men. You're no use to Major Anderson, or anyone else, dead. I'll get word to you if anythin' happens.'

Although the idea of running away galled Steve, he saw the sense in the editor's words. He strode towards the stables, where he found Corday in deep conversation with an even older man who was evidently the groom.

'What was all that shootin' back there?' Corday enquired.

'Two o' Clegg's killers tried to shoot me in the back,' Steve told him. 'Winton accepts that it was self-defence but figures I should get out o' town for a while.'

'You want company?' Corday asked.

Steve picked out his mount, shaking his head. 'Not this time, old-timer,' he said. 'Maybe this might not be a bad thing after all. It'll let me keep an eye on what's goin' on around the town. It's quite clear that very few of the townsfolk will talk to me. But there is somethin' you can do for me.'

'Name it.'

'It's possible these outlaws are slipping into town one at a time so as not to arouse any suspicions. Keep watch for any strangers who come in now and then.'

'I'll do that.'

Steve climbed into the saddle and threw some coins to the groom. Then he touched spurs to his horse's flanks and rode swiftly along the street towards the far edge of town. All the way he was acutely aware of the looks given him by the people on the boardwalks.

Perhaps, he thought, they had good reason to resent his presence there. Clegg sounded like the kind of man who would vent his fury on those people who lived on this side of the river.

4

NIGHT RIDERS

Seated on a smooth slab of rock, Steve scanned the whole of the western horizon. In that direction lay both Fenton and, further to the south, the Willard Flats. This was the second day since leaving the town, and in all that time the terrain had been empty. Now, with sundown only a few minutes away, he prepared to settle down for the night.

He had hoped that, from this vantage point, he might have spotted some activity around the town. But there had been nothing. He took out his bedroll and spread it on the hard ground.

A moment later, however, a faint sound brought him instantly alert. Crouching down behind a screen of bushes, he peered intently into the distance. The rider was approaching from the direction of the town and Steve's first intuitive thought was that Corday was out looking for him with news of some kind. Squinting against the glare of the rapidly vanishing sun, he gradually made out the indistinct figure.

When the rider came within 300 yards of his hiding-place, he realized that this was not Corday. This was a slightly taller figure, sitting easily in the saddle. Not until the rider was less than twenty feet away did recognition come.

Slowly, so as not to spook the horse, he rose to his feet. 'What the hell are you doin' here?' he demanded roughly.

Freya Morgan reined up her mount and stared down at him. 'That isn't a very polite greeting,' she said, slipping from the saddle. 'I thought I'd bring you some food and something to drink.' She untied the large sack tied to the pommel and dropped it on to the ground beside him.

'How did you find me?' The question came out more sharply than he had intended. But if she could discover him so easily there was no doubt Clegg or the outlaws could do the same and probably even more easily.

'That's no secret,' she replied calmly. 'You covered your trail well but Red Cloud followed it.'

Steve experienced a slight sense of relief. 'And where is Red Cloud now?'

Freya waved a hand in the direction she had come. 'He's back there less than a quarter of a mile away, watching the trail back into town. If anyone did follow us he'll give us plenty of warning.'

She lowered herself on to the rock beside him.

Quite suddenly, her expression changed. Grim lines furrowed her forehead. 'I also came to tell you that Ed Casson's dead.'

'Casson? The editor of the newspaper? But how did that happen?'

'More of Clegg's work. A band of his men were scouring the town, searching for you. When they couldn't find you, they went into Ed's place to question him. My guess is he refused to tell them anything, because they locked the door of his office while he was inside and then torched the place. There was no way he could get out.'

An intense feeling of fury rose up inside Steve, constricting the muscles of his throat. The news had stunned him. 'When did this happen?' he demanded.

'Some time during the early hours of this morning. The building was well alight by the time anyone noticed it and by then it was too late to help him.'

'But I suppose there's no proof that Clegg was behind it.'

'Everyone knows who gave the order.' Freya leaned forward, staring at the sun. Only the upper segment remained above the flat horizon. Already, darkness was hurrying in from the east. Her face bore a strained expression. 'But as you say, there's no proof. Even if there were any, he's got the judge in his pocket and there would be his men on the jury. He'd never be convicted.'

The anger still simmering inside him, Steve muttered, 'I'll make damned sure he swings for that – him and all o' the others who had a hand in it.'

They sat in silence as the dusk deepened around them. Then, suddenly, the silence was broken by a faint sound. Steve started to his feet, reaching for his guns. 'That sounded like a coyote,' he hissed.

Freya shook her head, getting lithely to her feet. 'That was Red Cloud. He's signalling that there are riders coming this way.'

'Then we'd better get the horses out of sight.' Steve caught at the bridle of his mount and led it towards the high bluff a short distance away. The girl followed him closely. Crouching down out of sight, they waited.

At first Steve could hear nothing but the wind murmuring among the rocks. Then he picked out the faint sound of approaching horses. Listening intently, he realized there was something odd about the gait of the animals. A moment fled before he recognized what it was.

The horses were not being ridden – they were being led. Moving slowly and carefully, he reached the edge of the bluff and peered around it. At first, he could make out nothing. Then he caught sight of the slow movement a couple of hundred yards away.

Three men were moving in single file, leading their mounts over the uneven, rocky ground, cursing loudly each time one of the horses stumbled.

Freya edged closer to him. 'Can you see anything?' she murmured softly.

Without taking his eyes off the approaching men, he whispered, 'Three men. They're leading their mounts and all of the horses are carrying heavy sacks. My guess is they're the outlaws and that's the gold from the army train.'

There was a pause, then Freya asked, 'Where do you think they're taking it?'

'It's hard to say. Somehow I don't reckon they've brought it out here just to bury it. They could do that anywhere. They've got some plan in mind or they wouldn't go to all this trouble. Whatever it is they're plannin' I need to find out.'

By now the trio of figures was passing the bluff. There was no indication on the part of the outlaws that they were aware of Steve and Freya's presence. Steve thought fast. Had he been alone he would have taken on all three of them but with the girl there, things could easily go wrong.

It was a measure of his concentration that he saw and heard nothing until Red Cloud was standing beside him, a dark shape in the deepening darkness. The Indian said something to the girl in a low voice, speaking in his own tongue.

'What did he say?' Steve asked.

'He said that those horses are almost at the limit of their endurance. They will soon be unable to go any further. If you wish, he will follow them to see what they intend doing with the gold.'

'All right.' Steve nodded. A few moments later the Indian glided away, a silent shadow in the surrounding darkness.

Less than fifteen minutes later he returned. Squatting down beside them, he said in broken English, 'They take gold to a small canyon not far from here. There is cave there in the side of the rock and they've placed the sacks in there and then covered the entrance with branches.'

'Where are they now?' Steve enquired.

'They mounted up and rode north,' replied Red Cloud.

'So why would they come all this way just to conceal it in a cave?' Freya's voice exuded puzzlement. 'Surely it would have been safer where they can keep an eye on it. It just doesn't make sense.'

'It does if that gold has been left there to be picked up by someone else,' Steve said. 'They can readily use any dollars they steal but gold is a different matter. Folk will start askin' awkward questions if you try to pay for anythin' in gold bars.'

'So you believe someone is coming to collect it?' Red Cloud asked.

'I'm sure of it and I want to find out who that someone is.' He turned to Freya. 'The two of you had better get back to town before you're missed by anyone. I'll keep watch on that gold. My guess is that some arrangement has been made for it to be picked up tonight.'

Freya made to protest but then fell silent, recognizing the wisdom of his words. She pulled herself smoothly into the saddle and, with Red Cloud trotting swiftly at her side, rode off in the direction of town.

Keeping hold of the bridle, Steve led his own mount into the rocks. As Red Cloud had intimated, he did not have far to go. Ahead of him was a narrow gully. On reaching the far end he found himself looking down upon a much wider stretch of smooth rock. On the other side a high wall of rock lifted some thirty feet into the cloudless heavens.

He readily made out the darker shadow and the thick branches that had been dragged across to it, totally concealing what lay behind. Very slowly, he edged back into the concealing shadow of the defile and settled down to wait.

Just over half an hour earlier Hal Clegg had ridden out with two men beside him. He knew that Minter and his companions would not dare to double-cross him. But ever since this stranger, who had shot down his men, had slipped through his fingers, there had been a deep unease in his mind. Just who was this man who had ridden unannounced into town? The only logical conclusion he had been able to reach was that the man was a state marshal, sent to hunt down these outlaws.

If that were the case, then his own plans could be in serious jeopardy unless he took swift and decisive steps to see that the stranger was eliminated. For a moment he wondered whether it had been a wise move to carry out that attack on the newspaper office. A lot of the townsfolk had had a whole heap of respect for Casson and he knew that the finger of suspicion would be pointed in his direction.

Not that he cared overmuch about what people thought of him. In his position it was inevitable there would be talk. There had been a lot of muttering when he had started driving some of the ranchers off their range but it had died down quickly once he had stamped his authority on the members of the town committee. Now he could put a lot of what was happening on to these outlaws just so long as none of them began talking to the wrong people. He was depending on Minter to keep the other two outlaws in check.

A mile or so from town he cut off the main trail and took a narrow track through the thick brush. The two men who rode behind him maintained a tense silence. By the time they came within sight of their destination darkness had fallen in earnest. The moon had just risen, round and full, over the distant hills. By its light, Clegg saw where the brush had been piled up to conceal the entrance to the hole in the rocks.

'It looks as though Minter has kept his word,' he growled as he dismounted and went forward. Signalling to his companions, he began stripping away the branches, unaware that a pair of eyes was watching his every move from less than thirty yards away.

From his vantage point among the rocks Steve recognized Hal Clegg right away. He smiled grimly to himself. This was all the proof he needed to place Clegg in with the outlaws. For an instant, the surge of anger he felt at the sight of these men threatened to overturn his reason. Every instinct told him to draw on them and shoot them down like the dogs they were.

But common sense told him that doing that would not solve his main problem – that of discovering where these outlaws were hidden. Every muscle in his body felt tensed and taut, but with an effort he fought to control his emotions. Lying flat on his stomach on the smooth floor of the defile, he kept still and watched as the men began hauling the large, heavy sacks out into the open.

Clegg stood a few yards away, occasionally throwing a searching glance back in the direction of Fenton. The man was clearly nervous, possibly sensing that something was wrong but not knowing what it might be.

He called suddenly, 'Hurry it up! We haven't got all night.'

'I don't see you helping,' grunted one of the men.

'I give the orders here, not you.' Clegg looked as if he meant to strike the man but, with a tremendous effort, he succeeded in controlling his anger and impatience.

At last the job was finished. The heavy bags were lifted on to the nearby horses and the two men stood waiting. Then one of them said, 'Where do we take this gold now, boss?'

'Back to the ranch,' Clegg ordered. He hauled his bulk into the saddle and waited impatiently for the other two to mount. In the bright moonlight it was obvious to Steve that, carrying all of that weight, they would have to make slow time back to their destination.

As the men rode off into the night, he reached a sudden decision. He eased his mount back along the defile, then climbed into the saddle and swung the horse round to follow the three men. He deliberately chose a trail some distance to the right of the one

Clegg was following. If any of them became suspicious, he would be easy to spot in the flooding moonlight. In places there was little or no cover and he had to drop some way behind.

Clegg seemed to be in no particular hurry now, nor did he keep turning his head to watch his backtrail. Five minutes later Steve saw the reason for the man's lack of concern. Three riders suddenly appeared from behind the shelter of a cluster of boulders.

Steve pulled his mount to a halt and waited. After a few minutes of conversation, Clegg moved on with the newcomers falling in behind him. Clearly, these were more of Clegg's men. In the sky the moon disappeared behind a large mass of dark cloud. Now it was no longer possible to make out the six men and he edged his mount forward at a faster pace. Then he spotted them again. They were about 200 yards ahead of him, cutting across a wide stretch of pasture.

Now Steve guessed where he was. This must be the wide strip of open range belonging to Clegg. Dimly, he picked out the stretch of barbed wire that divided it from the surrounding terrain. There was also something else.

Clegg had left one of his men behind at the gate leading on to his property. Narrowing his eyes, Steve took in every detail of the situation. So far, the guard had no idea they had been followed. He saw the yellow flare of a match as the man lit a cigarette. He was leaning nonchalantly against one of the posts.

Silently, Steve lowered himself from the saddle. Bent double, he moved slowly towards the wire. The gunslinger had his back to him, clearly unaware of his presence. Steve crept forward and pulled one of the Colts from its holster, reversing it and holding it by the barrel.

Noiselessly, he crept forward until he was right behind the man. Some instinct seemed to warn the guard of his danger. His right hand dipped downward for his gun as he half-turned, the cigarette dropping from his lips. An instant later, Steve's right arm came round in a vicious arc. The gun butt struck the man on the side of his head with a sickening thud. Without a single sound, he dropped face downward into the grass.

Steve holstered the Colt, then bent, grabbed the man's legs and hauled him to one side of the gate. A moment later, leading his mount through the gap, he was inside. Overhead, the moon sailed free of the dark cloud. In the distance he could just make out the loose bunch of men still moving away from him.

He breathed a sigh of relief and gigged the horse forward. Very soon the lights of the ranch house came into sight. The riders entered the courtyard and dismounted. Three of the men left, heading for the stables, while one remained behind with Clegg.

Steve stepped down from the saddle and led his mount towards a large clump of trees at the side of the house. Although they were speaking in low tones, Steve was able to pick out most of the words that passed between them.

'Get these bags stowed away in the barn yonder,' Clegg commanded. 'Make sure they're ready to be picked up once Gregson arrives. The sooner it's taken away, the better. That nosy stranger may still be hangin' around town and if he gets wind o' this, he could make trouble.'

'Why don't you let me and some o' the boys look around for him, boss?' asked the other man. 'It shouldn't be too difficult to flush him out wherever he's hidin'. Or are you hopin' those outlaws will take care of him?'

There was a slight pause, then Clegg said, 'My guess is those killers are planning another raid. They'll be too busy to bother about him at the moment. As for you and the boys goin' after him, that can wait until my own deal is completed. Gregson should be here within the next half-hour. He's been stayin' in town for the last two days. I want you to get this gold inside the barn and then watch the trail. Once he appears, bring him straight to me. You understand?'

The other man's reply was inaudible but a moment later he led the horses towards the barn while Clegg went inside the house. Steve led his mount further into the concealment of the trees and sat down on the thick grass. He had intended riding back into town to give this information to the sheriff but now he decided to wait and see just who this expected visitor might be.

He had already figured out that the gold was of little use to Clegg just sitting there in the barn. It might become common knowledge if he were to deposit it in his own bank. It wouldn't take long to figure out that the only place it could have come from would be that army train. Whatever happened, Clegg would have to be sure that his close association with these outlaws never became known.

Steve did not have to wait long. Less than twenty minutes later Clegg's hired hand arrived in the courtyard with another rider. As he crept forward to the edge of the stand of trees Steve was able to make out the man in the light streaming through the lower windows. He was a short, stout, man wearing a black frock-coat and a top hat. A thick black moustache adorned his florid features. Walking quickly as if he had no wish to be seen, the man followed his companion towards the house.

The door opened just as he got to it. Clegg stood there, silhouetted against the lamplight. He ushered his visitor inside and closed the door.

For a moment Steve hesitated, then he reached a sudden decision. Quickly, he made his way round to the rear of the building. The rear door was locked but one of the windows beside it had been left open. Clearly Clegg considered himself to be absolutely safe in his own home. It was the work of a few moments for Steve to open the window fully and climb inside.

He dropped lightly to the floor and peered about him. There was a door on the far side. He padded silently towards it and turned the handle slowly, opening it a little way. Voices reached him and, staring through the narrow crack, he found himself looking into the rear of the front parlour. Clegg was standing with his back to him, looking down at the other man who was seated in the chair by the window. They were evidently discussing the price Clegg wanted for the gold.

'That haul is worth at least fifty thousand dollars, Gregson,' Clegg was saying.

'Perhaps,' Gregson replied smoothly. 'But you must realize I have my own expenses. I have to be very careful whom I approach. Stolen gold is worth far less than the legal amount and since this is army gold, that will lower the amount I can offer you appreciably.'

'So what are you prepared to offer?' Clegg's tone held a hint of anger and disappointment.

'Thirty thousand dollars.' Before Clegg could argue further, Gregson went on swiftly, 'I'm prepared to take it now if you accept my offer. I'm sure you realize that the longer you keep it here, the more danger you're putting yourself into. The army won't wait to get their gold back and bring those responsible to justice. My advice is to accept my offer, which I assure you is final, and save yourself a lot of trouble.'

He tilted the glass of whiskey to his lips, then went on, 'I presume this is the gold from that train. May I ask how you got hold of it? I've heard rumours of outlaws operating in this territory – or perhaps all of this was your idea.'

'How it came to be in my hands is my affair and has nothing to do with our deal,' Clegg retorted. He paced up and down the floor a couple of times and then stopped directly in front of Gregson. 'Very well then. Thirty thousand dollars.'

'Good. We're agreed,' Gregson replied coolly. 'Now you're seeing sense.'

Steve backed away from the door; then stiffened. Something hard was thrust into his back and a rough voice said, 'Just hold it there, mister, or I'll pull this trigger. Now lift your hands.'

Cursing softly under his breath, Steve raised his hands.

'Now walk through that door and don't try anythin' funny.'

The two men in the parlour swung round in sudden surprise as Steve entered with the gunman behind him.

'Just found this *hombre* listening at the door, boss,' grated the man at Steve's back. 'I was knocked cold by some stranger at the perimeter gate just after you rode in with the others. When I came round I headed for the house to warn you and spotted this guy workin' his way round to the back.'

Clegg stepped forward, a bored smile on his fleshy features. Leaning forward, he jerked Steve's Colts from their holsters. 'Good work, Slim. This is that stranger who rode into town and killed two o' my best men. I figure we should take him into town and hand him over to the law.'

'You won't get away with this little scheme o' yours,' Steve said tautly. 'Folk will soon figure out what you're up to, working in cahoots with these outlaws. Once they know that and the fact that you had Ed Casson murdered it'll be you facin' the law, not me.'

'Oh, you're wrong my friend. I think you're workin' alone and once you're found guilty o' cold-blooded murder, when you shot my men in the back, you won't be around to testify to anything.'

Turning to Gregson he said tersely, 'I think it would

be better if you were to stay here for the night. As you can see, circumstances have changed. I need to get this man into the jail as quickly as possible before any friends he may have in town get wind of it.'

Ten minutes later, his hands tied behind his back, Steve was placed on his mount and was being taken back to Fenton with Clegg leading the way and four men riding behind him. He knew there was little he could do at the moment. What would happen once Winton heard of this, he wasn't sure. The sheriff knew he was working on behalf of the army but whether the threat of having troops enter the town would help him out of this tight spot was problematical. He didn't doubt that Clegg meant to have him hanged as soon as possible and there might not be time enough to get word through to Major Anderson before that happened even if Winton agreed to send someone to the fort.

There were few people about when they eventually rode into town. Those who were on the boardwalks looked the other way when they recognized Clegg.

'Get him down,' Clegg snapped as they reined up in front of the sheriff's office.

Two men pulled Steve off his mount. As he struggled to maintain his balance, he muttered, 'You won't get Winton to accept your trumped-up charge, Clegg.'

'Don't rely on him to back you up, mister.' There was a grin on Clegg's face as the door of the lawman's office opened and someone stepped out. 'Winton has had his day in Fenton. He's no longer the sheriff here.

Clem Halleran is the new sheriff.'

'And no doubt he's one o' your hired killers,' Steve muttered.

Clegg's grin widened even further. 'He was elected by the town committee by a unanimous vote.'

'I'll bet he was. A committee where all of the menbers take their orders from you. And what's happened to Winton? A bullet in the back or did you just run him out o' town?'

'What happened to him is no concern o' yours.' Clegg glanced up at Halleran. 'Put him in one o' the cells for the night, Clem. We'll try him first thing in the morning. No sense in wasting the town's good money on feedin' him until the circuit judge gets here. That won't be for another month.'

Halleran uttered a harsh laugh and stepped down into the street. He grabbed Steve's arms and thrust him up on to the boardwalk and through the door. He took a bunch of large keys from a hook on the wall and pushed Steve along a short passage at the rear. All of the cells were empty. Halleran unlocked one and gave Steve a hard push in the back, tripping him at the same time so that he fell painfully on to the floor.

With an effort Steve drew himself into a sitting position. 'Don't I get my hands untied?' he asked thinly.

'Sure,' muttered Halleran. 'When I say so.' He slammed the door shut and locked it before going back into the office, taking the bunch of keys with him.

Slowly, Steve managed to push himself up on to the

low bunk. He was in a tight spot and as far as he was aware no one was in a position to help him or even knew he was here. The cell was devoid of any furniture apart from the bunk on which he was sitting. There was no window, only four bare walls and the locked door.

Once he arrived back at his ranch, Clegg supervised the stashing of the gold bullion into the barn. He was feeling pleased with himself. Not only had he forced Minter to give him a third of all their proceeds from their robberies but he now intended to extract the highest possible price he could from the man sitting across the table from him.

'All right, Gregson, I know we agreed to a price of thirty thousand dollars but as I see it, circumstances have now changed a little.'

Gregson took a swallow of his drink, his features suddenly set into hard lines. 'I don't understand, Clegg. In what way have circumstances changed?'

Clegg smiled. 'I've now removed the only obstacle I had, that stranger who could have made things a little difficult for both of us, but especially for me. He's now locked up in the jailhouse and by tomorrow morning we'll have found him guilty o' murder and he'll be swingin' at the end of a rope.'

Gregson pursed his lips into a thin line. He toyed with his glass, staring down at it. 'I fail to see why that should make me change my mind. I've already told you that thirty thousand dollars is my final offer. Besides, from what little I saw of that man, he's still dangerous. How far can you trust this man of yours, whom you've just made sheriff, to keep him under lock and key?

'He knows far too much. Not only about your part in this scheme – but mine too. I say that as long as your prisoner's alive he's a danger to us. I'd feel easier in my mind if you were to send a bunch of your men into town right now, take him out o' jail, and string him up somewhere out o' town. Then we might discuss some slight incrcasc into what I'm prepared to give for that gold.'

Clegg ran a hand down his cheek. 'Two or three men would be enough,' he muttered musingly. 'I suppose you'd want to come with us?'

'Naturally. Just to make sure there are no mistakes. In my business, one must be extremely careful where every little detail is concerned.'

'Then if you're ready, I'll round up a couple of the boys.'

Almost an hour had passed and still Steve heard very little sound from the office at the end of the short corridor. But he knew Halleran was still there. Occasionally he heard the clink of glass and guessed Halleran was helping himself to Winton's whiskey.

Then he heard another sound. The street door opened and someone came in. There was the murmur of voices one of which seemed slurred, but whether it was Halleran or the newcomer Steve couldn't tell. After a moment he picked out Halleran's rough voice then came a crash as if something heavy had fallen.

Steve got to his feet and Steve moved to the door. What the hell was happening out there? he wondered. A few seconds later he had his answer as a familiar voice called, 'You in there, Landers?'

'Yes. In here.'

A shadowy figure appeared at the end of the passage and then Corday stood in front of him, a bunch of large keys in his hand. 'I figured you might need a little help,' he grunted. 'First Sheriff Winton is dragged out by some o' Clegg's men and taken out o' town and then I spot them bringin' you in. What's going on, Steve?'

'Get that door open and untie my hands,' Steve replied. 'There ain't much time. Someone may have seen you come here and gone to warn Clegg. I'll fill you in once we're well away from here.'

Corday tried a couple of keys in a lock before the third one opened the door. He pulled out a knife and sliced through the ropes tying Steve's hands. Flexing his fingers to restore the circulation, Steve followed the oldster into the outer office. Halleran lay on the floor behind the desk. There was a trickle of blood on the side of his face.

Corday took his Winchester from where it was propped against the desk. 'He weren't too bright, that one,' Corday said, grinning broadly. 'He figured I was drunk as usual and when he stood up to put me into a cell I hit him with the butt of Old Faithful here. Couldn't risk a shot but I reckon he'll be out cold for a few hours.'

'Thanks, old-timer. But now I think we'd better get

out o' here. The further we are from town before he comes round and raises the alarm, the better.'

'I brought a horse for you. It's tethered just around the corner. But I guess you'll need some guns so I brought them too.' Corday held out a gunbelt with a couple of Colts in the holsters. Quickly, Steve strapped it on.

Together, they went outside where Corday led him along the boardwalk and then round the nearby corner into a narrow alley. As the old man had intimated, a couple of mounts were tethered to a post. Within moments they were both in the saddle and riding swiftly along the trail leading out of Fenton.

It was fifteen minutes later when Hal Clegg rode in at the head of a small group of men. He noticed that the light was still burning in the office. Outwardly, nothing appeared to be wrong. Not until he thrust open the door and noticed Halleran lying behind the desk did the realization come that this stranger had somehow slipped through his fingers once again.

Rushing into the corridor at the rear he found the cell empty, the door open. Swinging on the men behind him, he stormed, 'He must've had an accomplice. Someone has got him out and by now he could be miles away.'

'If you'd killed him before bringing him here,' Gregson murmured, 'this would not have happened. Now that this man is once more at large, I think we will stick with our original deal. If you want to try for more than thirty thousand dollars, I suggest you contact someone else from New York. Somehow, I doubt if their offer will be as good as mine.'

Still consumed with rage, Clegg knew that Gregson had him over a barrel. He swung savagely on the two men standing awkwardly in the doorway. 'Bring this man round and then take him up to the ranch,' he snapped. 'I'll want to speak to him in the morning.'

5

DEATH AT MENDER'S CROSSING

By the time the three outlaws arrived back at Mender's Crossing darkness had fallen in earnest. Unaware of what was happening in Fenton, Minter was feeling pleased with himself as he stepped down from the saddle and followed the other two into the saloon. Butler lit a couple of paraffin lamps and set them down on the large table in the middle of the room.

As he threw himself down into one of the chairs, Iliff muttered, 'How far do you reckon we can trust this man Clegg, Matt?'

'About as far as he trusts us,' Minter replied. 'And that's only for as long as we need each other. We've no way of shifting that gold ourselves so we have to rely on him. At the moment, he holds most o' the aces.'

There was a long-drawn-out silence before Butler growled. 'What do we do now? Do you have any plans in mind?' He looked directly at Minter as he spoke.

Minter chewed on his lower lip for a moment. Then he said harshly, 'I've been thinkin' about that. It could be that things are getting' a mite too hot for us in this part o' the territory. Maybe we ought to consider movin' on.'

Butler took a grubby pack of playing-cards from his vest pocket and began thumbing through them. 'Why the hell should we do that?' he asked after a long pause. 'This is the best hidin' place we've come across for a long time. Nobody's goin' to find us here. Our faces aren't on any Wanted posters. Provided we're not seen together, we're free to wander around the town without anyone suspectin' anything.'

'What's your opinion, Will?'

Iliff took out a wad of tobacco. He bit a piece off and chewed on it slowly. 'I agree with you, Jim. There ain't any cause for us to move from here. We've plenty o' grub and whiskey. I say we stay.'

'Very well.' Minter leaned forward and rested his elbows on the table. 'Then here's my plan. The overland stage passes through Fenton twice every week. Now since we hit that army train, folk around these parts are wary about bringing in money for the banks in this region by the railroad.

'I suggest one of us rides into town tomorrow and gets some information on when they're carryin' that money. This time we just go for dollar bills. That way we won't have to bring in Clegg to take any gold off our hands.'

'Mebbe so,' Butler muttered. 'But he won't like it

and he'll still want his share.'

Minter smiled but there was no mirth in it. 'Then he can whistle for it,' he declared savagely. 'I'm getting fed up with him taking our dough and doin' nothing for it.' He straightened up. 'All right, it's agreed. Now who's ridin' into town tomorrow?'

'I'll go.' Iliff scraped back his chair and got up. He looked from one man to the other. 'Is that agreed?'

Both of his companions nodded. 'Just be careful who you talk to,' Minter warned him. 'After the attack on that train everybody will be careful who they talk to.'

'I'll watch myself.' He took a bottle of whiskey from the large sack on the table and moved away. 'Now I'm goin' to have a drink and then get myself some shut-eye.'

The sun was already high the next morning when Iliff gigged his mount along the dusty, empty street of Mender's Crossing. On either side, the broken windows stared down at him like empty eye sockets and there was no sound to be heard, no movement apart from a couple of buzzards wheeling in lazy circles high in the cloudless heavens.

Leaving the ghost town behind, he headed north across the sun-glaring emptiness of the Flats. Large tumbleweeds rolled aimlessly on both sides of him and an occasional sidewinder slithered across his trail.

Fenton came into sight almost an hour later and he reined up on a low rise, taking note of everything going on in the town. There seemed to be a lot of activity around the sheriff's office and as he watched Clegg came out, talking animatedly to the man beside him.

It was obvious something had happened during the

night, something he figured his two companions would want to know about. He decided to ask about this before trying to get information about the overland stage.

He rode slowly down the slope. The bright sunlight glinted brilliantly on the river where it flowed northward, dividing the town neatly into two. He tethered his mount to the rail on the opposite side of the street to the jailhouse and climbed up on to the boardwalk. There was a small knot of people talking among themselves in low tones.

'Looks as though somethin' mighty serious has happened,' he said to the man leaning on the rail beside him. 'What was it – a jailbreak?'

'Reckon so. Seems Clegg took away Sheriff Winton's badge and had his boys ride him out o' town yesterday. The town committee appointed one o' Clegg's men into office but we all know who runs that bunch o' spineless men.'

'Was that all? From here, Clegg don't look too happy.'

'He brought in a prisoner last evening and had him locked up in one o' the cells. Seems somebody went in, knocked this new lawman on the head with a rifle butt and set this *hombre* free. I reckon by now he'll be across the border, together with his accomplice.'

Iliff glanced across the street. Clegg was still talking to his companion, occasionally raising his voice in anger.

Turning to the man beside him, Iliff asked, 'Do you have any idea who this prisoner was?'

The man shook his head. 'Nope. They reckon he was some stranger who rode into town a few days ago.'

Iliff moved on through the small crowd that had gathered. He was careful not to let Clegg see him. At the moment he was in no mood to answer any awkward questions. Spotting the saloon on the opposite side of the street, he pushed open the batwing doors and went inside.

Even at that hour of the day the saloon was almost full of customers. Going over to the bar he turned and threw a swift, all-embracing glance around the room. He soon spotted the old man with white side-whiskers seated alone at the table in one corner. There was a half-empty whiskey glass in front of him.

The bartender moved along to stand in front of him. 'What'll it be, mister?'

'Two whiskeys,' Iliff said shortly. The barkeep gave him a strange look but said nothing. Iliff waited until they came, then asked in a low tone, 'Who's the oldster sitting alone in the corner yonder?'

The bartender flicked a glance in the direction of Iliff's nod. 'That's old Ben Travers. But if it's conversation you want, you won't get much out o' him.'

Taking the two drinks with him, Iliff crossed the room and sat down in the chair opposite Travers. He pushed one of the glasses towards the old man. 'Have this drink on me, Ben,' he said in a low voice.

The old man looked up and eyed him closely. Iliff's first impression that the oldster was touched in the head was instantly dismissed. There was an expression of shrewd intelligence in the bright blue eyes.

'Do I know you, mister?' Travers made no move to take the drink.

'Sure you do, but it was a long time ago when I was last in Fenton. You're Ben Travers, aren't you. My name's Iliff, Will Iliff.'

The other hesitated, then said, 'Guess my memory ain't as good as it used to be. Anyway, thanks for the drink, Will.'

Two more drinks and Iliff reckoned Travers was sufficiently drunk for his purpose. Leaning across the table, he said softly, 'I'm leavin' town on the next stage to Twin Springs. You got any idea when it gets in?'

Travers took another swallow of the whiskey, then nodded. 'Comes in around noon every Tuesday and Friday. The stage office is down the street a little ways from here. You can't miss it.'

'Thanks. I just hope it's well guarded, what with these outlaws runnin' wild in these parts.'

'Well, it ain't been held up yet, not even on the Fridays when they bring in those strongboxes with the money for the bank. After what happened with that army train I reckon they'll have even more guards ridin' with it.'

Iliff leaned back and rolled a smoke. It had been easier than he had expected, getting this information. So the stage with all that money on board was due to arrive here in three days' time. He tossed the last of his whiskey down, got up and left.

By now the crowd in front of the jailhouse had dispersed and the town seemed to have returned to its normal activities. There was no sign of Clegg or the men who had been with him. Leaning against the wall, he finished his smoke.

At the general store he purchased more whiskey and food before going on to the gunsmiths, where he got more ammunition. This done, he saddled up and rode back out of Fenton, highly pleased with what he had achieved.

Minter and Butler were seated on the boardwalk when he arrived back at Mender's Crossing. The sun was beginning to go down, throwing long, grotesque shadows across the narrow street.

'Well,' Minter said without looking at him, 'what did you find out?'

'Plenty.' Iliff licked a cigarette paper and rolled a smoke expertly between his fingers. 'It seems that Clegg caught that stranger who rode into town a few days back and tossed him in jail. Winton is no longer the sheriff. He's been run out o' town and one o' Clegg's men is the law now.'

He placed the cigarette between his lips, lit it and inhaled deeply, blowing the smoke into the unmoving air. 'The trouble is, somebody got into the sheriff's office durin' the night and freed this fella.'

Minter's initial look of satisfaction faded swiftly at this news. 'So he's still out there?' His fingers clenched into tight fists. 'This is all Clegg's fault. He should have shot this stranger while he had him. Now we've no idea where he is.'

'Yeah. But we can't be sure he's a lawman of some kind,' Butler put in.

'We'd be fools to take that chance,' Minter

snapped. To Iliff he said, 'What about the stage? Did you get the low-down on that?'

The other nodded. 'The stage with the strongboxes on board arrives in Fenton at midday every Friday. That should give us plenty of time to work out a plan. However, on that day it's heavily guarded so we might run into trouble.'

'All right. We'll start makin' plans tonight.' Minter wiped his face and forehead with a large red handkerchief. 'Thank God it'll be dark soon. This damned heat is beginnin' to get to me.'

Sitting on a log Steve spooned the hot beans off the plate, eating ravenously. Across the blazing fire from him Corday did likewise. They were hunkered down in the same wood where Steve had first met the old man. As far as they could tell they had not been followed from the town. In a way that worried Steve.

By now Clegg would have discovered Halleran and would know what had happened. It was possible he hadn't guessed who had helped him escape, and the lack of a group of men on their trail puzzled him. He didn't doubt that Clegg had been determined to hang him this morning.

Now he had escaped and was still as dangerous as ever. So what the hell was Clegg doing? Had something else come up that required his urgent attention – something to do with that man come to take the gold?

Glancing up from his meal, Corday muttered, 'You got somethin' on your mind, Steve?'

Nodding, Steve replied, 'Yeah. I would've expected

Clegg's men to have followed us from Fenton. It ain't like him to let us go without tryin' to hunt us down but so far we've seen nothing.'

'Then surely that's our good fortune.'

'Maybe so. But right now he'll be tryin' to figure out who helped me.'

'So?' Corday looked puzzled. 'I'm here with you, ain't I? If he's thinkin' straight, he'll know I'm the only one who could've helped you git out o' jail.'

Steve shook his head. 'There's the chance he might figure it was Freya Morgan. You can be sure he'll know she travelled to Fort Leveridge to see Major Anderson about getting help against these outlaws. He probably also knows we were talkin' together in the hotel. If he gets the idea into his mind that she helped me escape she'll be in grave danger.'

Corday shrugged. 'So what can you do, Steve? Even if you're right, it would be suicidal to ride back into town. They'd shoot you down on sight. Besides, she's a resourceful young woman with quite a few friends in Fenton – not least that Indian who's always with her.'

Steve wasn't convinced. 'Just the two o' them against Clegg and his men? They wouldn't have a chance. I reckon I—' He broke off sharply as a sudden sound disturbed the stillness.

It came from somewhere among the trees to their left. Slowly, they both got to their feet, guns drawn. Steve signalled to his companion to move away from the fire. A twig snapped with a sharp, explosive sound.

Then a voice called out from among the shadows, 'Hey there, the camp. I'm comin' in with my hands raised.'

Steve waited tensely, knowing this could be one of Clegg's tricks; that somehow he had located them and several of his men had already surrounded them. A moment later a dark figure entered the wide clearing, his hands above his head.

As the figure came forward into the firelight Steve recognized him at once.

'Lower your gun, Will,' he said, thrusting his own back into its holster. 'It's Sheriff Winton.'

'Ex-Sheriff Winton,' said Winton bitterly, lowering his hands. 'I sure didn't expect to find you here, Landers. I reckoned you'd be dead by now.'

He sat down beside the fire and now Steve could see that he was in bad shape. There were deep lacerations across his face and his clothing was torn in several places.

'What happened to you, Winton?' he asked. 'I heard that Clegg had stripped you of your job but. . . .'

Winton winced as he forced a smile. 'That was only the beginning.' He touched his cheek gingerly. 'They tied me by a length of rope to the back of my own mount and Halleran dragged me along the ground for a mile or so. Once he'd had his fun he cut me loose and left me in thorn bushes by the side of the trail.'

'So how the hell did you get here?' Corday asked.

'He spooked my horse, but that was his big mistake. I trained that bay from a yearling. It came back after he'd gone and somehow I managed to stay in the saddle until I spotted the smoke from your fire.'

'And where's your mount now?' Steve enquired.

'I left it near the edge o' the wood. Don't worry, it won't leave without me.'

'I reckon that Clegg and Halleran have got a heap of accountin' to do,' Corday said angrily. 'But I guess you must be hungry. I'll heat some more bacon and beans for you. Help yourself to the coffee.'

'Thanks. I could sure use some.'

Steve waited until Winton had finished before saying, 'I figure you'd best bring your mount here. Then you'd better decide on what you figure on doin' now you're no longer sheriff.'

Winton scratched his chin. 'I reckon that whatever Clegg and the town committee say, I'm still sheriff o' Fenton and I'll stay sheriff until the ordinary people vote me out of office. If neither o' you have any objections, I'd like to join forces with you. I still have my gun, but Halleran took out all o' the slugs.'

'We've plenty o' shells,' Steve told him. 'And you might be able to help me.'

'In what way?'

'As you know, my main reason for bein' here is to hunt down these outlaws. So far, nobody seems to have any idea where they're holed up. But I'm fairly certain it's someplace in the Flats. Do you know of any place where three men could hole up for quite a time?'

Winton's forehead creased in concentration. 'Can't say I've ever heard of any,' he said after a few moments. 'But there's a hell of a lot of country out there and most of it ain't been fully explored.'

'Well, wherever it is, there'll have to be buildings of some kind. I can't see those men livin' out in the open – certainly not in this blisterin' heat.' Steve noticed that Corday had been silent for some time.

Turning to the old man, he said tersely, 'You got somethin' in your mind, Will?'

'I'm not sure. Could be somethin', or it may be nothin'.'

'Whatever it is, spit it out. I'm willin' to listen to anything.'

Corday stared hard into the leaping flames 'Well, I've just remembered somethin' I heard quite a while ago while I was workin' with the pony express. This man maintained there was a trail that cut across the flats and the company had a big changing post out in the wastelands. What the hell was its name?'

He chewed on his lower lip. Then his face cleared. 'I recall it now. Mender's Crossing. It was almost like a small town with a couple o' saloons, a stable for the horses and several different stores. But there's nothin' left there now. The company ran a new route well to the north more'n twenty years ago. Mender's Crossing was left completely abandoned. Nothin' but buzzards and sidewinders there now.'

'But it would make a damned good hidin' place for these critters.' Steve turned the news over in his mind. It made sense. Almost all of the hold-ups had been within twenty miles or so of Fenton and the railroad was even closer.

'I guess I'll ride out into the Flats tomorrow and take a look around.'

Once out on the Flats, Steve allowed the sorrel to pick its own pace. Knowing nothing at all of the whereabouts of this long-abandoned town he had decided that his best approach was to ride along the rims of ever-expanding circles, thereby widening his area of search.

He passed a couple of ancient waterholes but they were as dry as a bone, their bottoms covered in a thick layer of fine silt. It was difficult to imagine that men had once been here, had build a staging post in this wilderness. How long this drought had lasted, it was impossible even to imagine. This was a part of the country where the rain came once or twice a century, leaving everything as dry as a bleached bone.

He experienced a brush of impatience in his mind. Inwardly, he felt absolutely certain that the outlaws' hideout was somewhere in this parched land but it was the sheer magnitude of the Willard Flats that impressed itself upon his mind.

Sometime just after high noon he came upon a ridge of prickly thorn and wild sage. It was the only vegetation that could survive in this wilderness. Here, almost the only movement was of the brightly coloured sand lizards that darted among the stunted bushes. An occasional scorpion scuttled across the alkali but his mount was a thoroughbred and gave these creatures a wide berth.

The day wore on slowly with the heat remaining at its peak, and he had still come across no trail to mark the recent passage of men and horses. He now rode with his neckpiece over his mouth and nostrils as the wind began to get up, hurling stinging grains of dust into his face.

But although little of it got into his mouth, it still

burned his eyes and he dared not rub at the itching film of dust on his face. It was so abrasive it would rub the skin raw in minutes. Narrowing his eyes to mere slits he turned his head slowly, scanning the entire horizon, looking for the faintest smudge that might indicate the presence of buildings. There was nothing but the shimmering haze.

By early afternoon he was becoming more and more convinced that this story of an abandoned township out here in the middle of this wilderness was nothing more than that. It was a ghost town that existed only in the imagination. He had already covered several square miles of territory without any success.

By mid-afternoon he decided to head back. It was senseless to continue searching with the heat at more than a hundred degrees. He had no fear of this country but the sense of caution that was something he always lived with overrode any further attempt to find this place.

Swinging his mount, he began to backtrack. Now the wind was behind him, whipping the dust into little eddies that chased each other across the undulating ground. He rode with his head lowered to keep out much of the glare, concentrating his attention on the ground under foot. What caused him to lift his head and look up at that moment was an instinctive action he did not fully understand. There was something in the distance to his left, something dark and irregular. In the shimmering, heat-laden air it was impossible to make out details or to determine whether it were real or just a mirage.

With a sudden surge of excitement, he pulled hard on the reins and touched his spurs to the mount's flanks. Even though it was clearly tired, the animal responded gallantly, its hoofs sinking into the soft, shifting surface with every step.

When he was still some distance away, he stopped and shaded his eyes against the brightness. At first he could make out little, but gradually details began to emerge. There were buildings there! Several seconds passed, however, before he fully realized he had at last found what he was searching for.

Mender's Crossing!

Now his natural caution came to the fore. He had no doubt in his mind that this was the hideout of the outlaws but the chances were that at least one or two of them were somewhere among those buildings. Those men might consider them safe from discovery but it would not be easy to approach the place without being seen.

There appeared to be very little cover between him and the nearest of the buildings. Easing the Colts in their holsters, he judged that he had no other choice but to ride for the edge of the town and trust to those men being inside, somewhere out of the heat. Spurring his mount forward, he raced forward, bending low in the saddle.

Mender's Crossing was larger than he had expected. It also appeared to be totally empty. There was no sound, no people on the dusty street that ran through the middle of it.

The battered, dust-scoured sign hanging outside the building right at the end of the street told him it had once been a gunsmith's shop. White dust lay in a heap against the wooden door where the wind had blown it over the years. He dropped from the saddle and tethered the horse out of sight from the street. Still there was no sign of life; no sound or movement anywhere.

He eased himself on to the rotting boardwalk and walked forward slowly, both Colts ready in his hands. There was still no sound to disturb the eerie stillness. Then, without warning, the wooden board beneath his feet snapped with a sharp, explosive crack. Caught off balance, Steve fell against the nearby wall. The next moment there came the sound of a shot. The slug gouged wood out of the boardwalk less than an inch from Steve's foot.

Instinctively, he threw himself down, peering through red-rimmed eyes to determine where the shot had come from. He could see nothing. Then, a second later, he caught sight of the man crouched down in the half-open doorway of the saloon on the other side of the street. Aiming swiftly, Steve fired. The man ducked back inside.

Throwing caution to the wind, knowing he was exposed to the other's fire if he remained where he was, Steve got his legs under him and darted across the street.

Two more shots rang out, the slugs kicking up dirt around his boots as he threw himself forward. He hit the boardwalk and rolled over, bringing up the Colts at the same time.

There was silence for a full minute. Then a harsh voice yelled, 'Just who are you, mister? How did you find this place?'

Steve pressed his lips tightly together and made no reply. Inwardly, he wondered where the other two outlaws were. Probably moving around to the rear of the saloon, he thought, hoping to pin him down from the other direction.

Now that he had committed himself he knew there was only one course he could take. Slowly, he levered himself upright, his back against the wall and edged towards the doors.

The rough voice came again from somewhere inside. 'Listen, stranger, there's no call for gunplay. There's money in here, plenty of it, enough for you if you want it.'

Steve guessed the killer was getting nervous now, but he was still dangerous. Pouching one of his Colts, he reached along the wall with his free hand and placed it flat against the outside of the door. Tensing himself, he thrust the door inward.

Three shots echoed in quick succession, the slugs punching slivers of wood on to the sidewalk. Sucking air into his lungs, Steve threw himself forward into the saloon, dropping on to his knees in the same fluid movement.

Another shot hummed dangerously close to his head, but in that moment he caught a glimpse of the muzzle flash. It came from the side of a stone pillar at the top of a curving flight of stairs leading to the upper rooms.

Running forward, he reached the bottom of the stairs. For a second, the man's head showed round the edge of the pillar Almost without taking aim Steve jerked up the Colt and squeezed the trigger. The next second the outlaw toppled forward, rolling headlong down the stairs to land at Steve's feet, his legs twisted oddly beneath him.

One glance was sufficient to tell him the other was dead. The slug had taken him right between the eyes. Turning away, Steve let his glance rove over the room, still alert for any sign of the other two men he knew to be in the gang. As the moments passed, the realization came to him that, for some reason, those others were not in the town.

There were still the remains of a recently eaten meal on the table and three empty whiskey bottles. He had no doubts in his mind that this was where these men were hiding out. He had discovered it only by chance. Going through the man's pockets he found little of any value – a pack of cigarette tobacco, papers and matches. There was nothing on him that might provide Steve with a clue to his identity.

He straightened up, walked to the doors and stepped outside. In the shimmering heat nothing else moved except for more buzzards circling lazily over the town. Wherever the others were they were clearly not here or he would have come under attack before now. Also, the sun was dropping towards the west and unless he wanted to be caught in the badlands after dark, he would soon have to find his way back to Cordray and Winton. The sooner this information was passed on, the better.

He whistled up the stallion, climbed into the saddle and rode out.

Earlier that day Minter and Iliff had ridden out of Mender's Crossing to take a look at the trail leading westward towards Fenton. Minter was fully aware that the stage would be well guarded and for him it was essential to pick the right spot for the hold-up. Making these preparations beforehand had worked well with the train and he had no intention of making any mistakes this time.

They came upon the trail almost two hours after setting out. It was merely a narrow strip of hard-packed earth but for several miles it ran across flat ground where there was little cover.

They eventually reined up their mounts at the top of a rise and sat smoking while Minter ran his gaze over the ground below them. 'There must be a better place than this,' he muttered under his breath. 'If we held it up here we'd be shot clean out o' the saddle within minutes.'

Eyes boring ahead from beneath thick brows, he ran his gaze further towards the east and then pointed. 'That might be better. Along there where it runs through yon hills.' He finished his smoke, tossed the butt away and wheeled his mount to follow the trail.

The bare hills were higher than they had thought: huge slabs of grey rock that in places rose almost vertically for 100 and more. Here a gap had been blasted through them and the trail ran for more than 200 yards between towering walls of stone. Minter nodded his head as he turned to his companion, a satisfied smile on his swarthy features.

'This is the place,' he declared emphatically. 'Plenty of cover and they won't be able to get behind us.'

Iliff nodded in agreement. 'If we hit them from both sides it should be easy.'

Minter urged his mount further into the deep cutting, scrutinizing the high walls of rock that hemmed in the trail. He rode for perhaps fifty yards, then halted and pointed.

'Here,' he called as Iliff joined him. 'It should be possible for a man to climb up there. It looks to me as if there's a ledge yonder. Someone there could find cover behind those boulders, wait until the stage has gone past and then hit 'em from the rear.'

Minter was feeling pleased with himself as he and Iliff rode back to Mender's Crossing. The sun was now going down, throwing long, black shadows across the ghost town. A little way ahead of him, Iliff suddenly reined up, staring straight ahead.

Drawing level with him, Minter asked, 'What's wrong?'

Iliff shook his head, his features twisted into a scowl. 'I don't know, Matt. But I don't like the feel o' this. There's somethin' not right.'

'Well, I don't see anything.'

They rode forward for another twenty yards before Iliff said sharply, 'Where's Jim? He's always sittin' on the boardwalk at this time, keepin' watch.'

'It's more'n likely he's lyin' drunk inside.'

Still wary, Iliff cupped his mouth and called loudly, 'Jim. Where the hell are you?'

When there was no answer the two men dismounted and walked slowly towards the saloon, their guns drawn. Cautiously, Minter thrust the doors open and went inside. The room was now shadowed and details were difficult to make out. Then Iliff uttered a sudden shout and ran forward, thrusting his Colt back into its holster.

'It's Jim,' he called gruffly. 'He's been shot.'

Minter ran forward and knelt beside the body. 'What the hell can have happened? It wasn't like him to allow anyone to get the jump on him.' He felt Butler's face. The skin was cold under his touch. 'He's been dead for some time,' he added.

'Could be he wounded his killer. He sure got off several shots since the doors back there are both splintered with bullet marks that weren't there when we left this morning.' Iliff's gaze probed every part of the room. 'I guess this means that we'll have to change our plans for the hold-up. We were dependin' on him.'

'I'll make my mind up about that in due time,' Minter snapped. 'In the meantime what worries me most is that somebody has found this place and knows we're here.'

'But who. . . ?'

'My guess is that stranger. You say he broke out o' the jail durin' the night and it's more'n likely he headed this way. He must've come upon this place by chance and run into Butler.'

'So what do we do now? We can't stick around here. By mornin' there'll be a posse out here surrounding the town.'

'Somehow I don't reckon so. Who's goin' to form a posse to come after us? Halleran the new sheriff?' Minter shook his head. 'I don't think so. He's one o' Clegg's men and he'll do exactly as Clegg tells him. There's no one this stranger can talk to.'

'Ain't you forgettin' one thing?'

'What's that?'

'He appeared in Fenton only a few days after we hit that train, so it's highly likely this *hombre* is workin' for the army. It's a day's ride to Fort Leveridge and the same back. In two or three days this territory could be overrun by soldiers.'

Minter thrust his face up close to Iliff's, showing his teeth in a savage grin. 'In three days' time we'll have that money from the stage and be over the border where they can't touch us.'

'And you reckon we can hold up that stage with just the two of us?'

'No reason why not, just so long as you keep your nerve. Besides, I've got an idea.'

6

HOLD-UP

Back inside the shelter of the trees Steve related to Corday and Winton details of what he had found. Both men listened attentively, not interrupting once. Not until he had finished did Winton say, 'That man you killed in that ghost town – you're sure he was one o' the outlaws?'

'Who else could he be?' Corday interjected.

Winton shrugged. 'Maybe he was just some panhandler who found a place to stay out o' the sun. You said yourself there were three of 'em, Steve. If that's so, where were the other two?'

Steve ran a finger down his cheek. 'That's what worries me. I doubt if they were in town. They never go there in pairs or the three of 'em together. Unless they'd gone to have words with Hal Clegg, my bet is they're plannin' something and the two of 'em had ridden out to check on the lie o' the land.'

He chewed slowly on his bacon, running over the various possibilities in his mind. After a while, he said, 'They've already hit that bank in Fenton once so it ain't likely they'll try to rob it again. Is there anythin' else they might decide to rob?' He looked across the fire at Winton.

'My God – yes.' Winton jerked the words out. 'Why didn't I think of it before? They'll be after the stage. It comes into Fenton tomorrow around noon bringing money for the bank and some o' the storekeepers.'

Steve gave a grim smile. 'Then I'd say we know their objective. The question is where's the most likely place they'd choose to hold up the stage?'

'I'd say that once it pulls out o' Clayton there's only one place along that trail that will afford them any cover,' Winton said as he tossed more wood on to the fire. 'Some twenty years ago a narrow pass was blasted through the hills east o' here. The trail passes through it. That would make an excellent place for an ambush. Plenty of cover and if they planned it right they could trap the stage where it would be impossible to move forward or back.

'There's also one other point we have to take into consideration,' Winton went on. 'As far as we know there are only two of 'em left. They'll need more men than that to take out the guards ridin' with that stage. Somehow they'll have to get more men to ride with 'em and that won't be easy. In the past they've always worked alone, just the three of 'em.'

Steve gave a grim smile. 'My guess is that if they

mean to go through with this hold-up there's only one man they can ask for help.'

'Who's that?' Corday looked up from the fire, an uncertain frown on his ruddy features.'

'Hal Clegg, o' course. We know he's been in cahoots with 'em for some time.'

'You reckon he'd even consider that?' Corday held out his hands towards the blazing fire. 'So far he's kept himself well into the background when it comes to bein' associated with these critters. Not only that, he'll soon know that you've found their hideout. Steve, and killed one of 'em. If he doesn't know already.'

'That's right.' Winton eased himself into a more comfortable position.

'If there's money to be had I'm quite sure he will.' the old-timer affirmed.

Corday's surmise was quiet right. Minter had already decided that he and Iliff alone stood little chance of holding up the stage even if they had the element of surprise on their side. He reckoned there would be at least a dozen, possibly more, men riding shotgun and accompanying the stage on its journey to Fenton. With Butler dead, he needed more help and there was only one person who was in a position to provide him with that.

Accordingly, an hour later, he rode back into town, heading straight for Clegg's ranch. There were still lights burning in the windows overlooking the courtyard. Two men were standing on the veranda smoking cigars.

Minter swung down from the saddle and knowing there were guns trained on him from the shadows, he approached the rancher.

Clegg spoke first and there was a certain vicious humour in his voice as he said, 'I've been expectin' you, Minter. I understand one o' your companions was in town a couple o' days back asking questions. Travers may be a drunken old fool at times but he knows that when I ask him questions he must always tell me the truth. I can rely on that.'

'So you know why I'm here?' Minter turned to stare at the man standing beside Clegg.

'It's quite all right to talk in front of Mr Gregson here.' Clegg blew a cloud of cigar smoke into the air. 'He's a friend from back East who is extremely useful in convertin' our gold into dollars. For a price, of course.

'But I'm sure you came here for a different purpose. You have somethin' on your mind and think that I might help. Is that not right? Perhaps you have it in mind to rob the stage tomorrow?'

Minter nodded. 'I'm quite sure it can be done and you, of course, would receive your share.'

Before he could go on, Clegg uttered a harsh laugh. 'That stage will be protected by more than a dozen armed guards. And you expect to rob it with three men?'

Minter hesitated. He was now feeling more unsure of himself than when he had started out. 'Two men,' he replied.

Clegg thick eyebrows shot up at that remark. 'Two?

So where is the third? Has he taken off with his share of what you already have?'

'Not exactly. Sometime this afternoon when Iliff and I were checking the trail for the best place to take the stage, someone shot him.'

Clegg's thin lips were pressed tightly together. 'You're tellin' me that someone now knows the whereabouts of your hideout?'

'It would seem so,' Minter admitted.

Clegg took a turn along the veranda, his hands clasped tightly behind his back, puffing furiously on the cigar still held between his thin lips. He came back to stand directly in front of Minter. 'You understand what this means? News o' that place could get out and if it reaches the army at Fort Leveridge, the whole o' this territory could be swarmin' with soldiers. That's the last thing I want.'

'It'll take two days for news to reach the fort and for soldiers to reach here,' Minter pointed out desperately. 'And it could take a week or more for them to decide what to do. In that time we'll have got everythin' that stage is carryin' and Iliff and me will be long gone. There'll be nothin' to connect you with us.'

'That's not the way I see it,' Clegg rasped. 'People in Fenton are already talking. It won't take 'em long to figure out I've been in on these robberies with you.'

Minter thinned his lips. He could see his hopes of getting some men from Clegg slipping away fast. Swallowing thickly, he said harshly, 'I'm prepared to give you half of what we get from that stage.'

Clegg hesitated at that and ran his tongue around his lips. He still recognized the danger he was in if anyone should get through to the fort and inform the army of what was happening in Fenton. But greed was slowly overcoming his fear.

'Half of everythin' you get?'

'That's right. And once we've divided it out, Iliff and I take off and you'll never see us again.'

'All right, Minter. It's a deal but you'd better stick to your end o' the bargain. How many men do you need?'

Minter pondered that for a few moments, then said tautly, 'Half a dozen o' your best gunmen should be sufficient. Just as long as they're men who'll carry out my orders without askin' any questions. I don't like the possibility o' getting a slug in the back and your men takin' off with the loot.'

'Believe me, that idea had never entered my mind,' Clegg said smoothly. He spoke the lie without any change in his expression. Changing the subject, he went on, 'I suppose you've already picked out the place where you intend to hit the stage?'

'Leave me to worry about that,' Minter declared. 'All I need to know now is where I'll meet you with your men.'

'Well, let's see. I presume you know the old trail out o' Fenton runnin' east from the town.'

When Minter nodded, Clegg went on. 'Very well. I'll bring half a dozen men with me and we'll meet you there at ten o' clock tomorrow morning. That should give us time to get into position.'

*

The three men rode slowly, eyes alert, in single file, along the narrow game track that led across the hills east of Fenton. They had left their camp in the wood almost an hour earlier. Here there was little cover and now they rode bent low in the saddle so as not to show much on the skyline.

A turmoil of thoughts raced through Steve's mind as he led the way. Was it possible they had misjudged those two outlaws? Maybe it wasn't the stage they had in mind. If that were so, he and his companions were out on a wild-goose chase while the killers were making ready to rob some other bank in the territory. There were so many imponderables to be taken into consideration when dealing with men like these. Taking into account the number of armed men who would be riding with that stage, it would surely be suicidal for two men to hold it up. Even with the element of surprise on their side, two men wouldn't have a chance against more than half a dozen.

From just behind him, he heard Winton call, 'Hold up, Steve. I thought I spotted movement yonder.'

Pulling on the reins, Steve brought his mount to a standstill. Winton moved up alongside him, pointing almost directly ahead. Steve narrowed his eyes and stared in the direction of the other's pointing finger. At first he saw nothing suspicious. Then he made out the small dust cloud.

'My guess is two men,' Winton remarked, 'riding the trail towards town.'

'That don't make sense.' Corday spoke up from a few feet behind them. 'If they're the two men you're after, Steve, why are they headin' that way? The stage will be comin' from the other direction.'

Steve pondered that for a long speculative moment, then shifted his gaze slightly. 'There's your answer.' He indicated a point some distance from the two riders. 'It seems we were right. Those must be Clegg's men.'

The second dust cloud was further away but over the minutes it became more clearly defined and it was obvious to the watching men that there were several riders in the second bunch.

'So Clegg is in on the deal,' Winton muttered.

'It would certainly look that way,' Steve nodded. 'And my guess is that Clegg is ridin' with 'em.'

'You reckon he'll risk his own hide if anythin' should go wrong?' Corday asked, keeping his gaze on the distant riders.

Rubbing the itching dust from his eyes, Steve said, 'Somehow, I doubt if he trusts his own men any more than he does those two outlaws. I figure he wants to be around when they take that money from the stage just to be sure he gets his share.'

In the distance, a little more than half a mile away, the two groups had met up and clearly there was some kind of conversation going on between them. Pushing his sight through the heat haze that was beginning to form, Steve was sure he recognized the bulky outline of Hal Clegg, but it was the figure beside the rancher that sent a shock of utter disbelief through him.

Reaching out, he grabbed Winton's arm, gripping it tightly. 'Do you see Clegg among that lot?' he hissed thinly.

Winton rubbed his eyes, staring across the intervening distance, a frown of concentration on his lined features. Then he gave a jerky nod. 'I see him,' he affirmed.

'Now take a good look at the rider on his left.'

Winton's eyes narrowed even further. The expression of concentration on his face suddenly changed to one of utter surprise and consternation. 'It can't be.' He muttered the words half to himself. 'It looks like Freya Morgan. But that's impossible. She wouldn't throw in her lot with those killers. Not after what happened to her father and Ed Casson.'

Steve gave an abrupt nod. 'I'm damned sure she wouldn't. That means she's there against her will. Somehow, Clegg has got a hold of her and brought her along as a hostage, just in case the stage guards get the upper hand. She's his insurance for getting away alive should anythin' go wrong.'

'Damn it to hell.' Corday spat the words out. 'He seems to have thought of everythin'. Only a polecat would bring a woman along to act as a shield.'

'They'll be movin' out soon,' Winton interrupted. 'It seems they've done with talking.'

The men had turned their mounts and were now heading away from town, moving at a steady pace. It was comparatively easy to pick out the slim figure of the girl among the riders. She was very close to Clegg and Steve was now reasonably sure there was a gun in the rancher's hand and that it was trained on her. The moment she tried to break away and escape, he would shoot her down.

'Right,' he said briskly, making up his mind at once. 'Now we follow them, but we keep our distance. Whatever happens, they mustn't see us.'

A sudden uneasy disquiet had descended upon Steve at the sight of Freya Morgan with Clegg. How the rancher had managed to kidnap her, he could not even guess. And more to the point, where was Red Cloud? What had happened to him? Whatever had occurred, it must have been sudden and taken both the girl and her constant companion completely by surprise.

Now her presence among that band of killers had added a new dimension to his problems. He didn't doubt that Clegg was not quite as sure of himself as he would like everyone to believe, otherwise he would not have need of this added insurance against failure.

With an effort he pushed these thoughts from his mind. Whatever happened, he needed a clear head if he was going to get her out of this alive. They were now riding through a deep arroyo with Winton picking his way carefully along the topmost rim, keeping watch on the riders in the distance.

A few minutes later the ex-lawman put his mount to the downgrade, sliding down in a cloud of dust. 'They've still no idea we're trailing 'em,' he said. 'Another fifteen minutes and they should reach that narrow pass through the hills.'

'And I'd say that's the only place along this trail

where they can lay an ambush,' Corday muttered. He tore off a piece from a wad of tobacco with his teeth and began chewing on it. His jaw working, he asked, 'So what do we do when we get there? We never expected to find the girl with 'em.'

'What can we do except keep a close eye on Clegg? The minute he makes a move towards Freya Morgan, he gets it. My guess is that he'll take no part in the hold-up. He'll stay well away from any bullets that might be flyin' around. All he's really here for is to protect his interests and make certain those two killers don't get away with all the money.'

They moved on, slowly and cautiously, until the narrow pass showed in the distance to their left. So far they had remained undetected by the outlaws but now there was a stretch of wide open ground between them and the trail.

'It don't look too easy to reach that pass from here,' Winton remarked grimly. 'There's no cover at all.'

'Yeah, but appearances can be deceivin',' Corday put in. 'There's a gully yonder. We can slip into it and get within a few yards o' the trail if we keep our heads down.'

Dismounting, they followed the old man. Less than a couple of minutes later they hit the gully just as Corday had said. It was almost four feet deep and the stone bottom suggested that it had once been a swiftly running stream. Without making a sound they lowered themselves into it.

Going down on to their hands and knees, they worked their way along it. Very soon, it was possible to hear the voices of the band of men ahead of them with Clegg's loud, booming voice raised above the rest.

'You three men move into the pass and find yourselves hiding-places among the rocks above the trail. And don't forget. Wait until the stage has passed you before you open fire. That way we'll have 'em in a trap.'

Freya's voice came clearly a few seconds later. 'You'll never get away with this, Clegg. That stage is too well guarded.'

'Oh, we'll get away with it. And if you've got any ideas o' tryin' to make a run for it, you'd better think again. You stay with me until this job is finished.'

'And then what?' Freya still sounded defiant even though she clearly knew the predicament she was in. 'You'll still have to kill me before I can talk. But you've no compunction about shooting an unarmed woman.'

There was a moment's silence and then the sound of a blow. 'Just keep your mouth shut. You're stayin' out o' sight with me once that stage comes. Keep quiet and you might stay alive.'

Gritting his teeth, Steve raised his head slowly, an inch at a time. There was a ragged sage bush on the lip of the gully and through it he was able to make out some details. Clegg was sitting his mount of the far side of the trail with Freya close beside him, sitting tall and straight in the saddle. Three of Clegg's men were just moving into the pass while the others had spread out on either side of it. He could see no sign of the two outlaws but a few moments later they emerged from the pass, one of them carrying a small reel of fuse in his hands.

Watching them closely, Clegg called, 'You know what you're doin' with that explosive, Minter? I don't want the pass blocked. We have to get into it to get the money.'

'I know exactly what I'm doin', Clegg,' Minter said harshly. 'This'll just bring a few boulders down on to the trail just in case the driver takes it into his mind to give the horses their heads and make a run for it.'

Bending, Minter struck a match and applied it to the end of the fuse. It sparked briefly as the men took cover. The explosions followed each other rapidly as several large blocks of rock fell into the trail just inside the pass. As the fumes settled, Minter walked forward and surveyed the results of his handiwork, nodded in satisfaction as he came back to the others.

'That should stop the horses,' he said loudly, 'but we'll be able to get round those rocks.'

'Good work,' Clegg called. 'Now all o' you keep an eye open for the stage. If it's on time it should be here within ten minutes. You all know what to do.'

Peering through the brush, Steve noticed that Clegg reached for Freya's bridle with his left hand, leading her back from the trail. That was enough to confirm his earlier suspicions – that he had a gun in his other hand. He knew that the rancher would not hesitate to use it to save his own skin if the gun battle went against him.

Lowering his head, he glanced back at Corday and Winton. 'They're all in position,' he said softly. 'Minter has blown a heap o' rocks down on to the trail at the exit, just enough to stop the horses bolting once they open up.'

'Those critters seem to have thought of everythin',' Winton growled, shaking his head.

'Mebbe so,' Steve conceded. 'But there's one thing they haven't taken into account.'

'What's that?' Corday queried.

Giving a grim smile, Steve replied, 'We're here and so far that's somethin' they don't know. If we take 'em from the side they'll be forced to divide their fire and it might give the guards with the stage the edge they need.'

He made to say something more but at that moment there came a sudden shout from just inside the pass.

'They've spotted the stage,' Corday muttered. 'Just give the word, Steve, and we'll pour hell into 'em.'

'All right. But keep your heads down.' Steve's mind was working quickly and clearly now. He withdrew the twin Colts from their holsters and checked that both were fully loaded. At his back, Corday had his Winchester ready.

A little further back still Winton held his guns ready, nodded as he felt Steve's gaze on him. Through tight lips he said, 'Clegg's goin' to regret the day he stripped me of my star. Now at last I've got the chance to even things up.'

Silence had now settled over the trail. Then they picked out the sound of horses and the creaking rattle of the stage in the distance. As the sound grew louder there was a sudden change as it entered the eastern side of the pass. Now the sound of horses and carriage wheels was accompanied by the echoes bouncing off the rock walls on either side. Judging by the sound, Steve estimated there were at least half a dozen men riding with it. To his way of thinking that meant there was more than the usual amount of money on board. It was evident that the outlaws had excellent sources of information in town.

Tensing himself, he waited for the sound of the first shots. When they came, he flinched in spite of the tight grip on his emotions. Men were shouting inside the pass and more gunfire broke out. Lifting his head, he looked across at the trail. Already, Minter and the others were on their feet and moving forward, guns in their fists.

'Are you both ready?' Steve muttered tautly. His two companions nodded. 'All right. Then let them have it.'

He pushed himself to his feet and aimed swiftly at two men running towards the entrance to the pass. One man died without knowing where the slug had come from. His companion dropped to his knees. Steve's second shot had hit him in the leg. He was sprawled on the ground but he was still dangerous. Holding himself up with one arm, the outlaw fired again and Steve heard the wicked hum of the slug as it passed within an inch of his head. Steadying himself, he made no mistake the second time.

The man reared backwards, his body arched into an almost impossible position, one hand lifted as if he were clawing at the sky. Then he slumped sideways, the weapon falling from his nerveless fingers.

Meanwhile the rest of Clegg's men had scattered, still confused by the suddenness of this unexpected attack. But now they were concealing themselves behind whatever cover they could find.

Clegg suddenly yelled, 'They're over yonder. It's that stranger and two others.' He raised his right hand and Steve's earlier suspicion was verified. He did have a gun and was covering the girl with it. Now, however, he began firing wildly in the direction of the three men.

He wasn't pausing to take proper aim but was urging his mount back from the trail, pulling Freya with him.

Inside the pass, out of sight of Steve and his two companions, the gunfire was now reaching a climax; deafening echoes reverberated into the distance, diminishing slowly. Steve guessed that the coach driver had spotted the debris ahead of him and had been forced to stop the stage. At the moment, however, there was no way he and his two companions could reach the pass. It would be suicidal to attempt to make it from where they were.

Swiftly, he cast about him for any possible way down. Looking to his right he noticed where it might just be possible to reach the top of the rocks where they overhung the narrow trail. Turning to Winton and Corday he snapped harshly, 'Keep me covered. I'm goin' to make a try for the top o' those rocks yonder.'

'Don't be a danged fool,' the older man grunted. 'They'll pick you off well before you get halfway to the top.'

'Just do as I say,' Steve retorted. He got his legs under him and hurled himself forward. It was at least ten yards to the nearest outjutting slab of rock. Behind him, his two companions opened up on the men below.

There came the vicious hum of a slug past his head as he sprinted across the treacherous ground. The ricochet plucked at his sleeve as he flung himself the last couple of yards, dropping behind the massive boulder. Gasping air into his lungs, he crouched there for a moment and then ran on again, hauling himself up from ledge to ledge. At any moment, he expected to feel the impact of a bullet but none came and, glancing down, he realized he was now out of sight of the men at the entrance to the pass.

Now the climb was more difficult, for there were few hand- or footholds in the smooth rock. Thrusting the Colt back into leather, he used both hands to get a better grip. Slowly, he inched his way to the top. Here the ground was smoother and, moving flat on his stomach, he pulled his way forward with his elbows until he could look down on to the scene below.

He readily made out the stage some twenty yards to his left. It was clear that both the driver and the man riding shotgun had been hit. From the way the latter was slumped forward, he guessed the man was dead. The driver, however, appeared to be only wounded for he still had a firm grip on the reins and was struggling to hold the frightened horses in check. All of this Steve took in with a single glance.

Then he quickly turned his attention towards the

rocks further along from him. Two of the ambushers had taken up positions there to enable them to fire upon the stage from the rear. The man on the same side of the trail as Steve was clearly dead. He lay head downward, his body draped grotesquely over the rocks. But his companion on the other side was still alive and firing at any targets that presented themselves.

Reaching back, Steve withdrew his Colt. The outlaw was cautious, showing very little of himself to the men below. Aiming carefully at the place where the other was concealed, Steve waited until the man raised himself to fire down at the stage. Then he squeezed the trigger. The impact of the slug knocked the gunman sideways. His weapon fell with a clatter down the rocks and a moment later his body followed.

Down below, Steve saw the coach driver turn his head, glancing up in surprise, wondering where the shot had come from. Steve raised a hand and saw the man nod in quick understanding.

Within minutes the firing died away completely. Steve ran along the top of the ridge until he drew level with the stage, then jumped down on to the roof of the coach, swinging himself inside. A woman crouched against the far window uttered a faint scream.

'You're safe now, ma'am,' Steve said. 'They're all dead except perhaps for one of the critters who master-minded this hold-up.' To the driver, he called, 'Once we get those rocks shifted from the trail d'you reckon you can drive the stage on into Fenton?'

'Sure, mister. It'll take more'n a flesh wound like this to stop me.'

'Good. I'll see how my two friends are doing. One of 'em used to be the sheriff in Fenton until Hal Clegg decided to take over.'

The man seated directly opposite Steve said harshly, 'You're tellin' me that Hal Clegg is mixed up in this business. I'm sorry, mister, but I can't believe that. I've known him for years and—'

'Then I guess you don't know him very well,' Steve retorted. 'He's been in cahoots with the outlaws in part o' the territory almost from the very beginning.'

Steve opened the stage door and climbed out. To him, it was now clear that Clegg's gamble with the two outlaws had failed. It was also clear, however, that it had taken its toll. Three of the guards riding with the coach had been killed and another, together with the driver, wounded.

Returning to his companions, Steve found that there was no sign of Clegg and the girl or Minter. Sometime during the battle the rancher had slipped away, realizing that his plan had gone wrong and that his own position was now precarious. Minter, too, must have realized that his only chance now was to ride for Mender's Crossing, collect as much of the money as he could carry, and try to reach the border before the law, or the army, caught up with him.

'Did anyone see which way Clegg went?' he asked grimly. Now his main fear was for the girl. Already, she knew far too much. While Clegg might be able to talk his way out of any complicity in the stage hold-up and conspiracy with the outlaws, he could only do that provided Freya Morgan no longer remained alive to give evidence against him.

'I reckon I saw him ridin' off in that direction.' Corday pointed towards the north. 'Guess he's headed back to his ranch.'

'Did he have the girl with him?' Steve knew the answer before the old man gave an affirmative nod.

'You goin' after them?' Winton asked. 'If you are, I'll ride with you. I have a score to settle with Clegg.'

Steve gave an emphatic shake of his head. 'Best I should go alone,' he replied. 'I know how you feel but one man has a better chance of getting into that place than two. My guess is he has to kill her to protect himself. Also, he still has plenty of men there to carry out his orders. Your place is here to help remove those rocks from the trail and let the stage through.

'Maybe once the townsfolk hear of what's happened from the driver, they'll realize just what kind o' man Clegg really is. A lot of 'em are still behind you.'

Steve ran back along the gully to where they had left their mounts. He climbed swiftly into the saddle, cut across the trail and headed north. Both anger and fear for the girl were now dominant in his mind as he rode, urging the stallion to as rapid a gallop as possible.

The animal responded gallantly, covering the ground in rapid strides but Steve knew with a sickening certainty that it would be impossible to overtake Clegg before he reached his ranch and even before that they would be inside his territory.

*

Clegg, meanwhile, was taking his anger out on his mount, lashing it furiously, still maintaining his firm grip on the rope tied to Freya's bridle. Her horse was not as fleet-footed as his and whenever he dragged savagely at it to force her to keep up with him he cursed loudly under his breath.

That stage hold-up should have been the easiest job in the world to pull off successfully. The plan that Minter had put forward had been an excellent one. With the men they'd taken with them it should have gone without a hitch. But then that goddamned stranger had appeared on the scene and everything had gone wrong. He had recognized the two men accompanying the gunhawk, whoever he was. Winton and Corday.

He now wished that he'd given orders for the lawman to be taken out of town and shot but it was too late for that. At least he had the girl and unless he missed his guess that stranger would do anything to ensure her safety. It had been a wise move on his part sending those two men to the house next door to the bank where Freya lived with just that Indian to keep watch. It had been tricky for his men but while one of them had grabbed the girl, the other had succeeded in knocking the Indian out cold.

A little while later they crossed the northern boundary of the ranch. Clegg drew in a deep breath while the man on guard opened the gate for him, then he said, 'It's just possible I'm bein' followed. If so, take care of 'em.'

The guard nodded and checked his rifle before closing the gate. 'You want me to kill 'em if they show up? Or do I bring 'em to the ranch house?'

'Kill 'em,' Clegg said coldly. He rode on without a backward glance, hauling Freya behind him. Not until he reached the safety of the courtyard did he feel a little easier in his mind. Now he had his men around him and as far as he was aware there were only three men against him and if they tried anything, they would be dead long before they reached the house.

Keeping the girl covered he turned to face Kenders. One look at Clegg's face told the foreman that something had gone wrong.

'Did everything go as planned?' he asked.

'No, it didn't,' Clegg snarled. 'That damned stranger showed up with Winton and Corday. They hit us from the side. Far as I know only Minter is still alive and he took off for that hide-out o' his in the Flats.'

'And what do you intend to do with me?' Her face still flushed with anger, Freya stared directly at him, eyes blazing. 'Shoot me out of hand like you've done all the others who've opposed you? Or perhaps it'll be a bullet in the back like my father?'

Holding his fury in with an effort, Clegg snapped, 'Sit down in that chair and keep your mouth shut.' To Kenders he said harshly, 'Find some rope and tie her down. If any o' those three men do get here, we'll push her up to the window where they'll have a clear view of her. If they fire on the house, she'll be the first to collect a bullet.'

Kenders went out and returned five minutes later with a length of stout rope. Clegg watched carefully as the man tied her into the chair with her arms behind her. When the man had finished he was satisfied that there was no way she could get out.

'Now round up the rest o' the boys. Bring them here. Pronto.'

Kenders left and Clegg saw him walking to the bunkhouse. Standing at the window, his hands clasped tightly behind his beck, Clegg pushed his gaze into the distance, along the narrow trail leading towards the town. In spite of his outward appearance of confidence in front of Kenders, he was more worried now than ever before in his life.

Things were not going his way at all. Something he hadn't considered before suddenly popped into his mind. Questions would be asked and once that stage arrived in town everyone would know who had been behind the hold-up. If that smooth-talking stranger turned everyone in Fenton against him, backed up by what the wounded driver had to say, his entire empire could come crashing down.

He took a cigar from his vest pocket and lit it, drawing deeply on it. With a sense of anger he noticed that his hands were trembling slightly. Savagely, he told himself he still had one ace up his sleeve – the girl. They wouldn't dare to attack the ranch house while he had her. If the worst came to the worst, he could use her as a bargaining tool, her life for the chance to take his money and ride across the border. With all the gold and dollar bills he had, it would be comparatively easy to start up again in some new town miles from here.

He swung round sharply as the men began to file into the room. Once they were all settled he said, 'We may have some trouble with that stranger who rode into town a few days ago. My guess is that he's already on his way here. I want every possible trail watched.'

'How many men does he have with them?' asked one of the men gruffly.

'Two – unless he succeeds in bringin' the whole town with him.'

Several of the men laughed loudly at this remark. 'You don't have to worry about him, boss. The townsfolk have no cause to go against you.'

'Unfortunately, things have happened that might change that,' Clegg told him. 'The stage hold-up didn't go as we planned. We lost several men but the driver and the passengers are still alive and they could testify against me.'

Kenders shook his head. 'Halleran is still in town and as far as the citizens are concerned, he's still the sheriff. I figure he'll stop any talk like that.'

Moving forward to stand in front of the men, Clegg gritted, 'I sure hope so. Now as I told Kenders here, I want every trail watched. Far as I know there are only three of 'em and I've told Jed at the outer fence to kill 'em if they show up there. Meanwhile, I'll keep an eye on the girl here.'

'You'll never get away with this, Clegg,' Freya said thinly. 'Landers will get you no matter where you try to hide.'

The palm of Clegg's hand came down hard on the

girl's face, the force of the blow knocking her head to one side. 'Don't bank on that. If he shows up anywhere near here, he's as good as dead.' Bending, he grabbed the chair and spun it round, pushing it towards the wide window. 'Just you sit there and watch him die.'

7

THE FINAL SHOWDOWN

The stage rolled into Fenton and pulled up outside the depot next to the sheriff's office a little over an hour after its scheduled time. Guessing that something had happened here along the trail, a small crowd had already gathered with Halleran and Sam Delman the mayor, in the forefront.

While a couple of men took down the dead guard beside the driver, a further two helped down the wounded man.

'What the hell happened, Jim?' Delman asked. 'Looks to me as though there's been a hold-up.'

Before the driver could make any reply, Halleran elbowed the mayor aside. 'This is a case for the law, Delman,' he said brusquely. 'I'll ask the questions.' At the moment, he wasn't sure what had happened but somehow he had the nagging suspicion that Clegg's plans had gone wrong. The rancher had ridden through the town earlier that morning with half a dozen of his men and he had also taken Freya Morgan with him.

He thought fast. It was unlikely that any of the passengers would be able to recognize Clegg's men. There would be little danger from any of them talking. But Jim Colter, the driver, was a different matter. He would almost certainly have caught sight of some of them and knew who they were.

Placing his arm around the wounded driver, Halleran moved towards his office. Over his shoulder, he called sharply, 'One o' you fetch the doctor. The rest o' you go back to your homes. There's nothing more to see.'

He took Colter into the office, kicked the door shut then lowered the driver into the chair facing the desk. The man was still conscious, his eyes open, as he stared up at Halleran. He ran his tongue around his dry lips. Throatily, he whispered, 'I know who staged that attack, Halleran. It was Clegg's men. He's workin' with those outlaws. I guess that means you're in on it too.'

Swallowing thickly, he went on, 'So what are you goin' to do now? You can't very well shoot me in here, not with all those folk still outside. So how are you goin' to keep me from talking?'

Thrusting his face close to Colter's, Halleran hissed, 'Nobody will believe you. This is all in your head.

Besides, I'm sure that Mr Clegg is a very generous man to anyone who helps him. Just think of it. No more drivin' the stage, riskin' your life every time you take it out. You could have a small ranch of your own. Live a much better life than you do now.' A note of menace entered Halleran's voice as he added, 'Accidents can happen all the time. Think it over and make your choice. Tell everyone the only men you recognized were those outlaws.'

At that moment the door opened and the doctor came in, carrying his bag. He set it down on the desk as Halleran straightened up. 'I've questioned him as to what happened,' Halleran said. 'He collected a slug durin' the gunfight. All he remembers is seein' the trail ahead blocked. As to the men who did it, all he can say is that he reckons it was those outlaws who've been plaguing the territory.'

'All right, Halleran.' The doctor jerked a thumb towards the door. 'You can go for the moment. If I can get this slug out there'll be no more questioning for a while. He'll need rest.'

Halleran pushed his way past the doctor, his gaze boring into Colter's. Outside, on the boardwalk, he raised his voice to a shout and yelled, 'It's all in hand now. All Jim can recollect is seeing two men he reckons must be those outlaws who attacked the bank here a little while ago.'

'You sure that Clegg ain't at the back of all this?' called a man at the rear of the crowd. 'There've been rumours goin' around that he's workin' with these outlaws.'

Halleran spun to face the man. 'I figure you'd better keep such thoughts to yourself if you know what's good for you.' He lowered his hands towards the gunbelt around his waist. 'Are there any more o' you who think the same way?'

Sullen-eyed, the crowd began to drift away. Halleran watched them go with a look of satisfaction on his face. He spun on his heel and went back into the office, where he found the doctor bandaging up Colter's shoulder.

'You figure he'll pull through, Doc?' he asked bluntly, aware that the stage driver's eyes were open and fixed on him with a half-frightened stare. He could guess what thoughts were running through the man's mind at that moment. Halleran reckoned Colter would keep his mouth shut for the time being but there might come a time when he had to be permanently silenced.

'So long as he doesn't exert himself I figure he'll be on his feet again in a couple o' weeks.' The doctor straightened. 'Does he have a place to stay?'

Halleran nodded. 'Just above the livery stables. I'll see he gets there.'

'Good. I'll take a look at him in a couple o' days.'

Once the doctor had gone, Halleran seated himself in the chair opposite Colter. He took a bottle of whiskey from the drawer in his desk, uncorked it and held it out to the stage driver. Weakly, Colter reached for it but the sheriff snatched it back before he could get his fingers around it. 'First you tell me exactly what you told the doctor.'

'I told him nothin'.'

'Are you quite sure about that? Like I told you earlier, Mr Clegg doesn't like people who talk too much about things that don't concern 'em.'

Halleran continued to stare directly at the other. Eventually he was satisfied that Colter had said nothing. He pushed the whiskey bottle across the desk. Colter grabbed it and tilted it to his lips. Then he put it back and wiped his mouth with the back of his hand.

From the top of a low hill Steve surveyed the land below him. His last incursion into Clegg's ranch had told him how difficult it would be to penetrate it, unseen, as far as the ranch house. It had got him into trouble then but now, with every man watching for him, it would be a hundred times worse. Yet if he was to rescue the girl, it was something he had to do.

The more he surveyed the rolling landscape below, the more convinced he was that he was missing something. There was the rich pasture extending almost as far as the ranch house, with Clegg's herd grazing on the lush grass.

In the far distance he made out the shape of the ranch house with the narrow sun-glittering river running behind it and then flowing on through the town. Somehow, he found his gaze drawn towards the river. That was his only chance. If there was one way in that might not be guarded, that was it!

He sucked down a deep breath and forced himself to marshal his whirling thoughts into some form of order. The ground immediately below him consisted of mainly open ground but just to his left the river flowed through a narrow channel. The banks on either side were high and laced with dense vegetation. He reckoned it would be possible to reach that stretch of rushing water without being spotted by any of Clegg's men. He took a drink from his canteen to ease his parched throat, then set the stallion to the rough downgrade, allowing it to pick its own pace.

He was now close enough to hear the turbulent rush of the water and so far there was no indication that anyone had seen him. But he knew there were men out there, sharp-eyed men, lying in wait for anyone heading in the direction of Clegg's ranch house. Ten minutes later he reached the thick brush that grew in wild profusion along the riverbank. Still there had been no sound of a shot. He had made it so far but the most dangerous part still lay ahead of him. The water was running swiftly down below him, channelled by the constricting walls of rock. It was not going to be easy moving through it, even though he would be moving with the current and not against it.

Dismounting, he grabbed the bridle and led his mount down the steep incline. The stallion was nervous but somehow he managed to calm it down. Fortunately, the river wasn't deep at this point. Nevertheless the sheer force of the current would make their footing precarious. Tugging hard on the reins he led the horse into the torrent. Immediately the sheer strength of the sweeping current hit his legs and it was only with a desperate effort that he managed to remain upright.

The surge of the river bore him forward, thrusting him irresistibly onward with it. The water came up to his waist and was icily cold, numbing his lower legs. About forty yards ahead of him the river angled sharply to his right, screened by the straggling bushes along the bank. Maintaining his tight grip on the reins, he made to go forward, then stopped instantly. There was someone else making his way along the river close to the opposite bank. Swiftly, he pulled the stallion to a halt, fighting the current all the time.

He recognized the man at once – Minter! He knew he couldn't risk a shot. The sound would be heard for miles in the silence and alert any of Clegg's men in the vicinity. Standing absolutely still, he watched as the outlaw staggered forward. He had left his mount somewhere before entering the river and there was a grim purpose in the way he forced his way forward.

Just what was the man doing here, moving in on Clegg like this? Steve wondered. He had expected Minter to ride out, out of the territory, after collecting as much of his ill-gotten gains as he could carry. He waited tensely until the other approached the rear of the ranch house before hauling himself out on to the bank. Minter paused there for almost a minute, peering about him for any sign of movement. Then he pushed himself to his feet and darted into the sun-thrown shadows.

This was something Steve had not anticipated. The only conclusion he could reach was that Minter intended getting more money from Clegg and had figured, like Steve himself, that this was the only way to get close to Clegg without being seen. Drawing in a deep breath, Steve pondered his next move. It was clear from Minter's actions that he had come here to have a showdown with Clegg. This was certainly going to make things even more dangerous.

Continuing his journey downstream, he soon reached the spot where Minter had hauled himself out of the water. Less than ten feet away was the rear of the ranch house. Once on the bank, he tied the stallion to a branch. There was no sound and he guessed that Minter was now somewhere inside the house. A couple of seconds later, however, there came the sound of a gunshot from somewhere inside. Moving along the wall, he came upon a large window that was open and he figured this was the way the outlaw had entered the building. It was the work of a few moments to ease himself over the windowledge into the room beyond.

Now he was inside it was possible to pick out the sound of raised voices. Steve knew at once who the men were. Clegg and Minter were in the midst of a furious argument. Making no sound, he padded towards the door on the far side of the room and opened it slightly. Now the sounds were clearer and came from the parlour at the front of the house.

Through the narrow gap in the doorway Steve made out Freya Morgan. She was sitting in a chair, her arms tied behind her back, facing the window that looked out upon the wide courtyard. He couldn't see either of the two men but a moment later, Clegg's corpulent figure came into view as he stepped up beside the girl, placing one hand on her shoulder. There was a Colt in his other hand and Steve guessed it was pointed at Minter.

He opened the door another inch, moved a little to one side, and now he could see the outlaw. Minter was lying against the wall and Steve made out the deep-red stain on the front of his shirt. There was a gun on the floor a short distance from him but it was too far for him to make a grab for it. Evidently the outlaw had come to kill Clegg but the other had been ready for him.

Clegg was saying, 'Too bad you had to let your greed get the better of you, Minter. I figured you'd be well on the way to the border by now.' There was a smug expression on Clegg's flabby features as he went on, 'I reckon that with both of your companions dead, I should lay claim to everything.'

'I'll see you in hell first, Clegg.'

'No doubt you will, but that won't be for some time yet. You're finished now. You don't even have the life left in you to go for that gun.'

'And you think the decent folk of this town are going to stand for it when they find out you've been in with the likes of him?' It was Freya who spoke this time, her voice dripping with sarcasm. 'They'll hang you from the nearest convenient tree first.'

Clegg swung his hand again, striking her viciously across the face. 'I told you to keep quiet,' he snarled. 'Another word out o' you and I'll kill you like this double-crosser here.'

Steve felt a sudden blind rage sear through him at what Clegg had just done. He reached down and made to slide the Colt from its holster, but before he could do so, a hand gripped his arm while another was slapped hard across his mouth. Even though he struggled against the hold it was impossible to break it.

Then the man who had him in the grip placed his head close to Steve's and whispered softly, 'Not a sound my friend, or he will kill Freya.'

Steve forced himself to relax. He recognized the voice at once. Red Cloud! Nodding to indicate that he understood, he felt the Indian's hold slacken and the hand was removed from his mouth.

Swiftly, he assessed the situation. It was clear that Clegg was now confident that Minter was finished. The outlaw was bleeding profusely from the wound in his chest and could not last out much longer. His own weapon lay too far away for him to reach.

Then Steve reached a sudden decision. It was not something he would have done under normal circumstances and he was relying on Minter's hatred of Clegg for it to work. The rancher now had his Colt pointed directly at Freya's head, the barrel almost touching her hair.

He took out one of his Colts and placed his other hand on the door in front of him. Swiftly, he pushed the door open, at the same time ducking and calling Minter's name. Both Minter and Clegg turned their heads. Before Clegg could recover from his surprise, Steve slid his own gun across the floor to where Minter lay propped against the wall.

The outlaw reacted as Steve hoped he would. Grabbing up the Colt, he swung sharply, bringing up the gun in a single movement, his finger hard on the trigger. The sound of the shot was like a clap of thunder in the room. Dying as he was, Minter somehow forced enough strength into his arm to fire off a second shot. Both slugs took Clegg full in the chest, driving him back against the window.

Glass shattered as he fell against it, his heavy frame lying across the windowledge, half-out of the building. Stepping forward, Steve bent and took his gun from Minter's fingers while Red Cloud checked on Clegg, then took out a knife and cut Freya free. She sat rubbing her arms and wrists where the rope had bitten into the flesh.

Against the wall, Minter stared up at Steve, a curious expression on his bearded features. 'Reckon you got everythin' you wanted.' Somehow, he got the words out. 'If it hadn't been for you, we'd have pulled it off. Even then this sidewinder. . . .' He inclined his head towards Clegg's body, 'tried to double-cross me and keep all o' the loot for himself. Now he's got what he deserved.'

A spasm of agony passed through him. He swallowed hard as he tried to say something more but there was no life left in him. A tickle of blood came from his mouth and dribbled down his chin as his head slumped forward on to his chest.

Steve went over to Freya and helped her to her feet. She swayed against him for a moment, then pulled herself together. 'He meant to kill me,' she said in a low whisper. She looked around her and there was still a hint of fear in her eyes. 'But his men will be here soon. They must have heard the gunshots. I heard him give them orders to watch every single trail leading to the ranch house. What are we going to do?'

'I reckon we've no chance of getting back to town. But with their boss dead I figure they're also finished here.'

Freya looked across at Red Cloud and there was an enigmatic expression in her dark eyes that Steve couldn't fathom. 'I have a feeling they'll be glad to pull out while they have the chance,' she said quietly. She seemed about to to say something more but the sound of approaching riders interrupted her.

A few moments later the first of Clegg's men appeared in the courtyard. Kenders was the first to swing down from the saddle. His right hand rested on the Colt at his waist as he called loudly, 'Everythin' all right in there, Mr Clegg? We heard gunshots and. . . .'

When there was no reply, he turned and signalled to the other men to dismount. Stepping forward beside Clegg's body, pressing himself close to the wall, Steve said loudly, 'Clegg is dead, Kenders. You can see him for yourselves.'

Before the foreman could speak, he went on harshly, 'And before you ask, it wasn't me who killed him. It was that outlaw, Minter. Clegg came back here with Freya Morgan. He intended to get out while the goin' was good and take the girl with him as a shield.'

'You're lying!' Kenders yelled.

He made to pull his gun, then paused as Steve said,

'I wouldn't try that. There are five guns pointed at you right now and you'll be the first to die. You're an intelligent man, Kenders. By now the stage will have reached town and my guess is that as soon as the truth is known, the whole o' Fenton will be headin' here and—'

Before he could stop her, Freya had moved to the window so that the men outside could see her clearly. Her voice rang out across the courtyard. 'My advice to all of you men is to ride out of this territory while you have the chance. Clegg is dead and you're no longer working for him. He can't protect you now.

'Furthermore, two days ago I sent my friend, Red Cloud, to Fort Leveridge with proof that your boss was working hand in hand with the outlaws. There's a troop of soldiers on their way to Fenton now. Somehow, I don't think any of you want to go up against them.'

Steve saw the men muttering among themselves as they digested this news. He didn't doubt that Freya was telling the truth. Clegg would never have been able to kidnap her if the Indian had been around.

He made a quick decision, knowing that now was the time to seize the initiative. Calling to Kenders, he said, 'You – shuck your gunbelt and come inside. Once you know the truth I reckon you'll accept what Freya Morgan has just told you.'

He saw the big foreman hesitate. Going on quickly, Steve called, 'I've got no quarrel with any of you men. By now, all o' the men I came out here for are dead.'

Slowly, Kenders unbuckled his gunbelt and let it

drop. After throwing a quick glance at the rest of the men in the courtyard he strode towards the front door, thrust it open, and came inside. He was still wary as Steve kept his Colt trained on him.

Pointing towards the smashed window, Steve said tightly, 'There's your boss. Like I said, I didn't kill him. Minter yonder got here before I did. I could hear them quarrelling from the back room yonder. Then there was a shot and when I looked inside, Minter had been shot and was already dying.'

'Then how did the boss come to be shot by that outlaw? Unless I'm mistaken, that's Minter's gun on the floor.' There was a note of disbelief in his gruff voice. 'He could never have reached it before Clegg shot him again.'

Steve grinned mirthlessly. 'I slid my gun to him. When I called his name Clegg took his attention off him. It was only for a few seconds but long enough for Minter to get in that last tellin' shot.'

Kenders' lips thinned down into a straight line. 'All right,' he muttered at last. 'I reckon you're tellin' the truth, mister. I suppose there's nothin' here for any of us now but we're all due back pay even though Clegg is dead.'

Shrugging, Steve said, 'Take whatever is owed to you and then ride out. There'll be a lot more useless bloodshed if you stick around. Either the townsfolk will get here or maybe the soldiers from Fort Leveridge will reach this place first.'

Ten minutes later the men rode out, heading north, away from Fenton. Steve went outside and sat down on the veranda drawing deeply on a cigarette. Freya came to stand beside him. Placing one hand on his shoulder, she asked, 'What do we do now? The townsfolk will have to know what's happened here. God alone knows what lies Halleran has been spreading around.'

Steve reached a decision. 'First we take those two bodies into Fenton and have them taken to the morgue. I'm hopin' that the driver of the stage is still alive. His testimony alone will be enough to prove that Clegg was in with those outlaws.'

They brought a couple of horses from the stables and hoisted the bodies of Hal Clegg and Minter across the saddles. All the way to the outskirts of Fenton they saw no one. Evidently those had been all of Clegg's men and they had taken the opportunity to get out of the territory before the army arrived.

Curious stares followed the trio as they rode along the main street to the sheriff's office. Steve reined up his mount and called loudly, 'Halleran! Get out here.'

There was a pause, then the door was flung open and Halleran stood there. He ran his glance over the three riders, then drew back his lips across his teeth. 'So you finally decided to give yourself up. Somehow, I figured you'd keep on running and—' He broke off sharply as he caught sight of the two bodies draped across the horses.

Stepping down, he looked up into the faces of the two men across the saddles. A look of utter consternation flashed across his face as he straightened slowly. 'It's Hal Clegg and one o' those strangers who used to come into town for food,' he yelled to the watching crowd. 'Both shot – and I'd say we have the killer right here.' He swung round and jerked his thumb towards Steve.

'You can't talk yourself out o' this, Halleran,' Steve said thinly. 'Clegg shot Minter, probably in an argument over how to divide the gold they got from the army train, but before he died, Minter killed Clegg. I was there and saw it all, as did Freya Morgan here. Clegg had her tied to a chair, ready to kill her the moment I showed up. They were also the ones who held up the stage this morning. Ask Jim Colter if you haven't already killed him. He can testify to that.'

Halleran looked wildly about him, saw the dawning comprehension on the faces of the onlookers. Before Steve could even guess at what the man intended to do, Halleran had snatched Freya from her mount and held her in front of him as he drew his Colt, thrusting it hard into her back.

'All o' you stand back,' he hissed venomously. 'I'll plug her the first wrong move anyone makes. Now I'm goin' to whistle up my horse and ride out o' here with the girl.' He grinned viciously. 'I reckon you'll all do as I say if you want her to stay alive.'

Gritting his teeth, Steve watched helplessly. He knew only too well that a speeding bullet could outmatch any move he made for his gun. All eyes were now fixed on Halleran as he gave a shrill whistle.

A few seconds later, two things happened simultaneously. Halleran's mount came from around the side of the sheriff's office – and a single shot rang out. With a low cry, Halleran reeled backwards, his gun hand jerking upwards. His shot went harmlessly into the air as Steve raised his head, staring over the crowd.

Caught up by the drama being played out in front of them, no one had noticed the two riders approaching along the street. Winton swung down from his mount and walked over to where Halleran lay, face up, in the dirt. Bending, he ripped the silver star from the dead man's shirt.

Glancing the direction of the mayor who was standing among the knot of onlookers a few feet away, Winton said tautly, 'I'm takin' this star back, Mayor. I reckon it's been sullied long enough by this critter here.'

Pinning the badge on to his shirt, he said authoritatively. 'Some of you take Halleran along to the morgue. In the meantime, I'm appointing Will Corday here as my deputy.'

There were murmurs of surprise from some of the crowd but no one made any objection. Slowly, the onlookers began to disperse. A couple of men picked up Halleran's body and carried it along the street to the morgue.

Steve looked around to find Freya's eyes on him. Her lips curved into a warm smile and there was something in her eyes he had never seen before. 'I suppose that ends it all now as far as Fenton is concerned. With Hal Clegg dead and all of his men gone, the ranchers he drove off their land will get it back.'

Nodding, Steve replied, 'I guess you're right and your father's death has been avenged.'

She came right up to him and took his hand in hers. 'With your job here finished, will you be riding on now?'

'Somehow, I don't think so. Now that Winton is sheriff again, I figure there can be law and order here. Like most frontier towns, Fenton could grow into something big, a town where a man could stop moving from one place to another and settle down.'

Smiling, Freya murmured, 'That's what I think too.' Without turning her head, she called, 'Don't you think it's time you and your deputy got down to some work, Sheriff Winton?'